Enjoy all of these Am

THE SILENT STRANGER   A *Kaya* Mystery

LADY MARGARET'S GHOST   A *Felicity* Mystery

THE TRAVELER'S TRICKS   A *Caroline* Mystery

SECRETS IN THE HILLS   A *Josefina* Mystery

THE RUNAWAY FRIEND   A *Kirsten* Mystery

THE HAUNTED OPERA   A *Marie-Grace* Mystery

THE CAMEO NECKLACE   A *Cécile* Mystery

SHADOWS ON SOCIETY HILL   An *Addy* Mystery

CLUE IN THE CASTLE TOWER   A *Samantha* Mystery

THE CRYSTAL BALL   A *Rebecca* Mystery

INTRUDERS AT RIVERMEAD MANOR   A *Kit* Mystery

CLUES IN THE SHADOWS   A *Molly* Mystery

LOST IN THE CITY   A *Julie* Mystery

and many more!

— A *Rebecca* MYSTERY —

A GROWING
SUSPICION

by Jacqueline Dembar Greene

Special thanks to Judy Woodburn

Published by American Girl Publishing
Copyright © 2014 American Girl

Questions or comments? Call 1-800-845-0005, visit **americangirl.com**,
or write to Customer Service, American Girl, 8400 Fairway Place,
Middleton, WI 53562-0497.

Printed in China
14 15 16 17 18 19 20 LEO 10 9 8 7 6 5 4 3 2 1

PICTURE CREDITS
The following individuals and organizations have generously given permission
to reprint illustrations contained in "Looking Back": pp. 156–157—photo by
Antonio M. Rosario (Japanese garden); Photography Collection, Miriam and
Ira D. Wallach Division of Art, Prints and Photographs, The New York Public
Library, Astor, Lenox and Tilden Foundations (women with flower arrangement);
pp. 158–159—Jacob A. Riis / Museum of the City of New York (urban garden);
courtesy of Jacqueline Dembar Greene (Children's Garden sign);
pp. 160–161—courtesy of the Brooklyn Botanic Garden, Louis Buhle, greenhouse
class on starting roots and bulbs, 1915; photo by Antonio M. Rosario
(contemporary children gardening); courtesy of Special Collections and Archives,
Furman University (woman in kimono); Stereograph Cards Collection, Prints
and Photographs Division, Library of Congress, LC-USZ62-121061 (Japanese
teahouse); The Walters Art Museum, Acquired by Henry Walters, 1904 (vase);
pp. 162–163—courtesy of the Brooklyn Botanic Garden, Louis Buhle,
view from west shore, 1925; Japanese hill-and-pond garden, photo by
Antonio M. Rosario; cherry trees in bloom; photo by Antonio M. Rosario;
garden statue, photo by Antonio M. Rosario.

Illustrations by Sergio Giovine

Cataloging-in-Publication data
available from the Library of Congress

To Ken and Doug,
wizards of Hudson Valley Seed Library,
saving gardens one seed at a time

TABLE OF CONTENTS

1
A BACKYARD MYSTERY

Rebecca ran her finger lightly over the shiny green leaves sprouting in pots on Ana's kitchen windowsill. "What are these?" she asked her cousin.

"I'm growing cucumbers," Ana said proudly. "And I think these plants are ready to go outside. I'm going to have a wonderful garden!"

"You're planting a garden?" Rebecca asked. "This Brooklyn apartment is so different from where you lived on Orchard Street. There sure wasn't any space for a garden there."

Ana gave a little shudder. "I wish never to go back to that terrible tenement," she declared. "Here, there are windows in every room and lots of light. I have my own bedroom, and Josef and Michael have a room, too, instead of

1

sleeping on the floor. Mama loves this big kitchen so much, she's always humming while she cooks. We even have a bathroom *inside* the apartment."

Seeing how well Ana and her family were doing gave Rebecca a warm feeling. Living in Brooklyn had given them a new life. Rebecca knew how hard they had struggled to escape from Russia, and how difficult life had been when they first arrived in America. The family was crowded into a dark, stuffy tenement on the Lower East Side, and Uncle Jacob and Ana's brother Josef had been forced to take terrible jobs in a clothing factory. When Uncle Jacob and Josef joined a workers' strike trying to make working conditions better, they were fired. For a while, the future had looked desperate.

Things had finally improved now that Uncle Jacob had a new job as a carpenter and his family was living in Brooklyn. But it was a long trip on the subway from Rebecca's row house to cousin Ana's new apartment.

"I miss having you nearby," Rebecca told her.

Ana wrapped her arms around Rebecca and gave her an exuberant hug. "We may not live close, but we'll always be as close as twins," she said. "And now we have one whole week of school vacation to be together!"

Rebecca was filled with anticipation. The week also promised to be wonderful because Aunt Fannie had offered to teach the girls to make a special recipe. "I can't wait to learn how to make *knishes*," Rebecca said. "When I get home, Mama will be so surprised—and the twins are going to be perfectly jealous!"

"Nothing's more fun than cooking together," Ana said.

"Well, there's something else almost as good," Rebecca added, smiling slyly. "Sadie and Sophie have to stay home and mind Benny, while for once, I'm the one who gets to do something special."

Ana laughed.

"It's true!" Rebecca insisted. "Just because the twins are older, they get special privileges while I'm stuck at home looking after Benny.

Just think of all the extra chores Sadie and Sophie will have this week."

"I'm afraid I have some chores for you, too," said Ana. "Would you help me with my garden? I have to clear out the weeds and dig straight rows so I can plant these seedlings." She handed Rebecca two cucumber plants and picked up two more.

"I've never weeded before," Rebecca admitted, "but as long as we do it together, it will be fun."

"I wish you could stay forever," Ana said.

"Me, too!" Rebecca agreed as the pair headed down the stairs and outside into the mild April air.

Ana led Rebecca down the wide front steps of her brick building and around the side to the back, where a low iron fence enclosed a sunny yard. Ana pushed open the gate with her elbow.

"Papa said the fence will help keep rabbits out of the garden," she explained. "There are lots of rabbits around here!"

"I've never seen one near our row house,"

Rebecca said. She glanced around the open space. It was larger than any yard in her neighborhood. Clotheslines stretched from each of the three apartments in Ana's building to a row of trees growing along the left side. A strange low box with a glass top sat on the ground near her feet. Farther back, a wooden shed with bright white shingles stood close to the fence, with a heap of rotting grass and leaves piled beside it. Just in front of the debris was a small plot of dirt with neat rows set in arrow-straight lines.

"This looks like a perfect yard for a vegetable garden," Rebecca observed. "So where are the weeds?"

Ana's mouth dropped open as she approached the rows of neatly mounded dirt. "Just yesterday, there were weeds everywhere," she said. "Weeds don't just disappear." She surveyed the yard carefully, and her eyes fell on a dented bucket near the shed. "And neither do tools! I left my hoe next to the bucket so we could get to work, but now it's gone—and my spade's gone, too!"

A GROWING SUSPICION

"They must be here somewhere," said Rebecca, setting down the cucumber seedlings. "What does a hoe look like?"

Ana put down the pots she was carrying and walked around the yard, her eyes on the ground. "It has a long wooden handle and a metal piece on the end to dig up weeds. Papa found it lying in an empty lot next to the apartments he's working on. How will I ever get another one?"

"Maybe someone put your tools away in there," Rebecca suggested, pointing to the shed.

Ana shook her head. "I was using that shed to store them, but a few weeks ago I found the tools on the ground and the door padlocked. I had to start leaving them outside."

"Maybe the landlord doesn't want tenants using it," Rebecca suggested. "I wonder why not. Tools don't take up much space." She walked to the shed and tugged at the lock, but it wouldn't budge. When she let go, it thudded against the wooden door with a hollow sound.

"Who would take an old hoe and spade?"

Ana wondered aloud. "Even though Papa cleaned off most of the rust and rubbed the handles with oil, they were worn out."

"Maybe someone borrowed them to start his own garden," Rebecca said. "I'll bet the tools turn up soon." But she had her doubts.

Ana went over to the low wooden box Rebecca had noticed. "Well," she said, "the only thing we can do now is put these seedlings in the cold frame." She leaned down and propped open the glass top with a stick. Inside, Rebecca saw pots of seedlings sending out their leaves.

"Papa built this for me," Ana said with a note of pride. "He used some leftover planks to make the sides and an old window for the top. The glass lets the light come through and keeps the plants warm even when it's cool outside. I keep the lid closed when it's cold, and when it's really sunny I open it a bit so the plants don't get too hot. They could die if it's too warm or too cold." Ana poked a finger into the dirt in each pot.

Rebecca peered into the box. "Where did you get all the seeds?" she asked.

A GROWING SUSPICION

Ana brightened. "A lady named Miss Ward came to our classroom and showed us how plants grow. She talked about vegetables that we could grow ourselves. Then she gave everyone seeds to take home." She pointed to some sprouts with dark, shiny leaves. "These are peppers," she said. "That's cabbage, and these thin green shoots are chives." She collected the cucumber seedlings and nestled them into the cold frame. "When these grow, Mama's going to make pickles!"

"Don't they need to be planted in the ground?" Rebecca asked.

"That's what I was going to work on this week," Ana said. "I thought it would take a few days just to weed the rows and loosen the dirt." She bit her lower lip. "How can I plant without tools?"

Rebecca didn't know what to say to make Ana feel better. It sure seemed as though someone had taken the tools, and she didn't really think they would turn up again. Anyone mean enough to take Ana's tools certainly wouldn't have weeded her garden. It didn't make any sense.

"A neat garden grows the best vegetables," said a soft voice behind them. Rebecca was startled to see a man step from the deep shade of the building.

"Mr. Tanaka, you're as quiet as a shadow!" Ana exclaimed, smiling at the man. She turned to Rebecca and said, "This is our neighbor, Mr. Tanaka. He and his wife came all the way from Japan. They helped us so much when we first moved in. Mama says she doesn't know what she would have done without them."

The short, muscular man bowed slightly and pushed his glasses back up on his nose. The thick lenses magnified his brown eyes, and fine wrinkles crinkled at the corners. "It's difficult to get settled in a new place," he said. "I know it was hard for us." He nodded toward the tidy garden rows. "But you are doing quite well now, young Ana, and I see that your garden is almost ready for planting."

"I really didn't do anything," Ana protested.

A GROWING SUSPICION

"When we got here, the weeds were gone, and so were my tools. Have you seen anyone around?"

Mr. Tanaka shook his head. "Every day I go to work. If anyone came into the garden, I wouldn't see." Then he looked questioningly at Ana. "Your tools were quite old, weren't they?"

Ana nodded. "Especially the hoe."

The man tapped his forehead as if suddenly remembering something important. "Perhaps it is the *tsukumogami*."

"What?" the girls asked in unison.

Rebecca tried to pronounce the unfamiliar word. "What is a soo-koo . . ."

Mr. Tanaka carefully sounded out each syllable. "You say *soo-koo-moe-gah-mee*. In Japan, we tell stories of a sprite that lives in ancient tools. Tsukumogami will do the tool's work if it is well cared for. This is a favor to its respectful owner." He lifted his eyebrows. "Perhaps the sprite was pleased and did your work while you were away. Now it is off taking a rest." He walked toward the gate, steering the girls ahead of him.

"Maybe we'll start putting the plants in the ground, then," Ana said, looking back. "My cousin is staying for the whole week, and we can get a lot done." She set her mouth firmly. "I'll dig the holes with my fingers if I have to."

"First, this poor soil needs to be fed," advised Mr. Tanaka. "Plants cannot grow strong without good dirt."

Ana pointed to the mound of debris Rebecca had seen at the far corner of the yard. "Papa and I made a compost heap with all the leaves we raked up last fall. We've been throwing in eggshells and potato peels, and even used tea leaves. Now Papa says it's turned into 'black gold'— the best soil ever." She frowned. "If I could just find my hoe, we could start mixing that into the rows."

"It is still too early to plant tender seedlings," Mr. Tanaka cautioned. "Today, the warm April sun can fool you. By tomorrow, everything could be frozen. Wait until May. Perhaps your tools will come home by then," he said encouragingly, urging the girls out through the gate.

"And maybe your tsukumogami will fertilize the garden, too."

Rebecca chuckled. "There can't really be a tool sprite. Someone must have done the work and then taken the tools."

Ana glanced back at the garden with disappointment. "I really wanted to work on the garden myself," she explained. "That's the fun of having it!"

Mr. Tanaka looked at Ana thoughtfully. Then he pulled a flyer from his pocket and unfolded it. "Perhaps you'd like to learn more about gardening. Did you know that I work at the best garden you can visit? It is called the Brooklyn Botanic Garden."

"Mama mentioned you were a gardener," Ana said uncertainly.

Mr. Tanaka straightened his shoulders. "My wife and I were brought here from Japan by the famous garden designer Takeo Shiota. I have helped build a Japanese garden that is a place of calm and beauty. My wife works there as well, welcoming visitors to the teahouse."

Rebecca wasn't sure what a Japanese garden looked like and had never heard of a teahouse, but it all sounded interesting. She peered at the flyer and read the words aloud:

Vacation Week Special!
Gardening Workshops for Students
Age Twelve and Older
10:00 a.m. until 3:00 p.m.
Fee: Ten Cents

"I'm afraid we can't take those classes—we're only eleven," Rebecca said with disappointment. "Anyway, where would we get two whole dimes?"

"I have an idea," Mr. Tanaka said. "You seem willing to work, and I could use some helpers. Perhaps you two can come to the Japanese Garden with me and my wife this week, and we will help you learn about gardening. In return, you can help with some small tasks."

Ana clapped her hands together with delight. "I'll ask my parents," she said. Turning to Rebecca, she added, "My vegetable garden will be the best one in Brooklyn!"

The girls waved good-bye to Mr. Tanaka and hurried up the steps of Ana's building. Rebecca felt caught up in Ana's enthusiasm, but she couldn't help wondering: *Who had taken Ana's tools, and who had done her gardening?*

2
GARDEN GUESTS

"I thought you wanted to bake knishes tomorrow," Aunt Fannie said. "Now, is more exciting to go see a garden?"

"Not more exciting, Mama," Ana said carefully, "but it's a chance for me to learn more about gardening. I want to grow lots of cabbages and cucumbers for you!"

"Could you teach us to make knishes when we get home?" Rebecca asked.

Aunt Fannie considered for a moment. "I think maybe our neighbors are missing their own young *boychik*," she said finally. "Maybe they feel not so sad if they can enjoy a day with two sweet girls."

Ana looked concerned. "Where is their son? Did they have to leave him in Japan?"

A Growing Suspicion

"I thought you knew," Aunt Fannie said. "I am sorry to share this story, but boychik died just before they came to America. He was same age as Michael. I am not understanding Mrs. Tanaka so good, but sounds like he died of fever."

"How sad," Rebecca said. "They must miss him so much. We'll try to cheer them up tomorrow."

"That's a *mitzvah*," Aunt Fannie said, smiling. "So then is settled. You go to garden in morning, and then you come home and together we are making knishes!"

The next morning, the girls waited just a few minutes on the corner before the Tanakas joined them. As they approached, Rebecca couldn't take her eyes off Mrs. Tanaka. Slender, and barely taller than Rebecca herself, the gardener's wife moved gracefully along the sidewalk in delicately embroidered slippers.

Instead of a typical shirtwaist and skirt, she wore a pale lavender *kimono* that reached the tops of her feet. It was tied with a wide purple sash and was lovelier than any costume Rebecca had ever seen. The flowing sleeves on the kimono reminded her of a butterfly's wings.

"She's beautiful," Rebecca whispered to her cousin.

"Please meet my wife," Mr. Tanaka said.

"Glad to meet you," the girls said in unison.

Mrs. Tanaka bowed and murmured, *"Konnichiwa."*

Rebecca guessed that must be the Japanese word for "Pleased to meet you," or perhaps "hello." It hardly mattered. Mrs. Tanaka was so captivating that Rebecca began to picture her as the star of a movie, with lavish sets and costumes. Ever since she'd had the chance to play a small part in a moving picture with Mama's cousin Max, there was nothing Rebecca loved more than acting.

"Normally, my wife would wear a kimono only on special occasions," Mr. Tanaka explained, "but when she greets visitors at the teahouse, she must reflect the image of a traditional Japanese woman. Each day, she also demonstrates the art of creating flower arrangements called *ikebana*."

The girls nodded. Rebecca couldn't guess what such flowers looked like, but she was sure they must be beautiful.

On the way to the Botanic Garden, the trolley sped along Flatbush Avenue, past spanking-new apartment houses, small shops, and shiny motorcars that sputtered and honked as they passed by. Rebecca barely noticed. Instead, she stole glances at Mrs. Tanaka. The gardener's wife kept her eyes lowered and didn't say a word.

Maybe she doesn't speak English, Rebecca thought. She knew it had been terribly hard for Ana and her family to learn English when they first arrived. Aunt Fannie and Uncle Jacob still often spoke Yiddish, their own first language. But Rebecca didn't need to have a conversation with Mrs. Tanaka to admire her flowing

silken robe and the wooden hair combs that
fastened a sleek bun at the back of her pale neck.
Mrs. Tanaka was lovelier than any of the real
actresses Rebecca had met. She envisioned
herself starring in a moving picture, costumed
in a flowing kimono just like Mrs. Tanaka's. The
movie would be titled *The Gardener's Wife* . . .
and naturally the poster advertising it would
feature her.

Rebecca was shaken from her fantasy when,
after just a few stops, Mr. Tanaka stood abruptly.
He escorted his wife and the girls off the street-
car and through the black iron gate of the
Brooklyn Botanic Garden. Immediately, Rebecca
felt as if she had entered a magical space. Trees
bursting with lime green buds lined the path,
and in every direction she saw low shrubs with
purple blossoms and patches of vivid yellow
daffodils set off by clusters of bright blue
flowers.

It was as if she had been transported from
the bustling city into another world. "I thought
we were going to see an ordinary flower

garden," she said, "but this is like stepping into the Emerald City!"

Ana reached for Rebecca's hand and gave it a soft squeeze. "It really is as dreamy as *The Wonderful Wizard of Oz*," she murmured.

"I think Mr. Tanaka must be the Wizard," Rebecca whispered.

Together, the girls followed the Tanakas along the broad dirt path to a low, white-painted building surrounded by a large unplanted garden plot. A tall woman stood near the front door. She wore a long gray skirt with a thick woolen sweater buttoned over her shirtwaist. Her hair was pinned up in a sweeping pompadour.

"Oh," Ana murmured. "That's Miss Ward, the woman who came to my class."

Miss Ward looked up from her clipboard. "Good morning, Mr. and Mrs. Tanaka. Are you bringing some new gardeners to my workshop?" she asked brightly. "The Children's Garden is almost ready to plant."

"Good morning," said Mr. Tanaka, pressing

his hands together and giving a short bow. "My young neighbors love to garden, but they are not yet old enough for your class. Instead, I plan to show them around the Japanese Garden and have them assist me this week."

Miss Ward's expression clouded. "That would be highly irregular. Children shouldn't be in the garden without supervision."

"I will look after them and keep them busy," he explained, pushing his glasses up. "They will learn quickly."

Miss Ward stared pointedly at the cousins until Rebecca squirmed. "You certainly could not find a better tutor," she said at last. "Mr. Tanaka has been the backbone of the Japanese Garden area." She gave a soft laugh. "I do believe he can predict when every leaf will sprout and every bud will bloom.

"If you are willing to assume responsibility, Mr. Tanaka, perhaps we can try it out just for today." Then she addressed the girls. "I hope you young ladies will not keep Mr. Tanaka from doing his job. Lately, some unfortunate incidents

have added to the work here. Just last week
a cluster of irises was torn out near the pond.
It was difficult for Mr. Tanaka to save them."
Miss Ward shook a finger sternly at the girls.
"Although you're not in my workshop, you must
follow the same rules as the students. Be sure
not to interfere with Mr. or Mrs. Tanaka," she
cautioned, "and don't wander off on your own.
Stay on the paths at all times, and do not pick
so much as a dead weed unless you're told to."

Rebecca swallowed hard. She hadn't expected
a gardening teacher to be stricter than her
teacher at school!

Ana didn't seem at all bothered. "You're so
kind to let us stay," she said politely. "I remember you from your visit to my class. I've already
started all the seeds you gave me, and I'm plan-
ning a backyard garden. You don't need to
worry about us for a moment. We'll do exactly
what we are told."

Miss Ward's face softened. "All right then,"
she said. "If you show me that you are responsible young ladies, perhaps I will make an

exception and allow you to join a class this summer."

"Oh, thank you," Ana said, beaming at the offer. "If I could, I know I'd have the best garden in Brooklyn—not counting this one!"

Rebecca felt a tiny pang of jealousy. "I'm afraid I won't be here in the summer," she said. "I'm only visiting this week." Still, she truly hoped her cousin would be able to join a workshop. Ana seemed to love growing plants as much as Rebecca loved acting.

The girls hurried along behind the Tanakas as they started off again. Rebecca marveled at each neatly tended flower bed and perfectly pruned bush. Nothing seemed to be in need of repair. The garden was bursting with new leaves and buds. It truly was an Emerald City.

Then, just ahead, Rebecca saw a sparkling building constructed entirely of glass. Its rounded roof arched gracefully against the blue sky, the panes of glass glinting in the morning sun.

Mr. Tanaka held the door open and beckoned

the girls inside. Rebecca stepped into a warm, sunlit space filled with lush, green plants from floor to ceiling. She took a deep breath. The air smelled sweet and delicate, like Mama's special bottle of perfume.

What a perfect place to film a moving picture! Endless light poured in from every angle—just what a movie camera needed. On the movie set, she had learned that artists had to paint artificial flowers on glass plates if they wanted to create a garden scene. This glass house was overflowing with real flowers. The imaginary movie popped into Rebecca's head again. The lovely young gardener's wife would work in a place like this!

"Walk around and enjoy the orchids and tropical plants," Mr. Tanaka said, "and I'll put away your lunch." He took Ana's school lunch box and disappeared into a storage room, closing the door behind him.

The girls wandered among the displays, admiring the colorful flowers. A stream trickled and flowed into a miniature pond filled with lily pads, and it was all indoors! Rebecca was so entranced that she barely noticed when Mr. Tanaka returned wearing a blue smock with large pockets. He pointed to a slender tree with a smooth green trunk, enormous leaves, and a fat cluster of green fruit hanging upside down. "What do you see?" he asked.

"Oh!" Rebecca gasped. "I had no idea that's how bananas grow!"

Ana reached over and cautiously touched a green banana. "There must be thirty in one bunch!" she marveled.

"We will come back later," Mr. Tanaka said. "First, I will show you my masterpiece." He smiled mysteriously as he led the girls back outside. The chill morning air felt fresh against Rebecca's cheeks after the moist warmth of the plant house. Mrs. Tanaka followed silently, cradling several long flower stalks in her arm. Their spiked orange and blue blossoms looked almost like the silhouette of a bird.

The girls followed Mr. Tanaka up a gently sloping path. When Rebecca turned a few moments later, Mrs. Tanaka had turned down another path. Rebecca wished she could have gone with her to the teahouse to see what she would do with the spiky, birdlike flowers.

The path opened onto a wide grassy walkway bordered by a few spindly trees bursting with pink blossoms. Mr. Tanaka swept his arm in an arc. "Below us is the Japanese Garden, planned in every detail by Mr. Shiota, my illustrious teacher. It is just one small section of the Botanic Garden, but it is a world apart. I helped place every flower, tree, and rock, down to the smallest pebble. Each one feels like a familiar spirit."

"Like the *soo-koo*," Rebecca whispered to Ana. They giggled softly, but Rebecca felt a tiny shiver at the thought of the sprite working unseen, like a busy ghost. She reminded herself that it was just a story.

Mr. Tanaka stroked the smooth bark of a small tree. "This cherry tree is just a sapling now, but someday it will be part of a vast cherry orchard. While the trees are young, I prune and shape. In time, they will grow to match each other. Every spring, cherry blossoms will color the path like a painting." His eyes gleamed.

Below the hill where they stood lay a pond. Cherry tree branches drooped over the water's edge, casting a pink reflection. Rising from the water in the center of the pond was a startling sight—a huge crimson arch topped with thick wooden beams that curved upward at the ends.

As Mr. Tanaka led the girls around a bend, they came upon a tall stone lantern set in a patch of ferns. "When candles are lit inside," he explained, "the pathway glows."

Just as Rebecca was trying to imagine the lantern lighting the path at night, a flash of purple made her turn. Below her, Mrs. Tanaka was crossing a bridge with wooden railings carved into a design. The reflection of her kimono and her blue and orange flowers made the rippling water shimmer with color.

Mr. Tanaka paused at an arched door in a wall made of bamboo. He lifted its large iron latch and pushed it open. "Come," he said. "Inside is a secret."

3
A SECRET GARDEN

On the other side of the bamboo door, Rebecca saw a small area that looked at first like a shallow pond, its surface stippled with rippling waves. But instead of water, she realized, the waves were made of pale, coarse sand. A cluster of boulders was arranged near the center, and a few stalks of tall grasses offered the only hint of color. At the back, a stone bench nestled against a whitewashed wall topped with red clay tiles.

"This is my sand garden," Mr. Tanaka said. A hint of a smile curled the edges of his mouth. "It is an artful design that makes us imagine water. The large rocks are like an island."

"Why is it a secret?" Rebecca asked.

"This is a small example I have made to show

A SECRET GARDEN

Mr. Gager, the director of the Botanic Garden. I am hoping to create a larger sand garden for visitors to enjoy, but right now, the director says this does not fit his budget. Perhaps one day soon he will feel its beauty and want many people to enjoy the peaceful space."

"Can we climb on the rocks?" Rebecca asked.

Mr. Tanaka shook his head. "A sand garden is a place to sit and let one's mind rest. It isn't for visitors to walk upon. But you are going to walk upon it right now—for a special task."

He retrieved two long-handled rakes, each with a straight row of thick wooden tines, and handed one to each of the girls. "The sand must be raked daily to keep weeds from taking root and to smooth the wave pattern. I do not want Mr. Gager ever to find it in disarray. If you groom it, you will save me much time and earn your keep today." He smiled. "It is a challenging task that takes experience to do well. Still, I would like you to try. Perhaps you will see how peaceful it is." Then he turned and walked out, closing the door behind him.

A Growing Suspicion

Rebecca and Ana stepped to the back of the garden. They each began raking from a different direction but quickly discovered it was not as easy as it had first seemed.

"Careful," Rebecca cautioned. "You're stepping on my waves."

"I can't help it," Ana replied. "I have to walk across that spot to reach this side." She set to work, trying to fix the spots where she had stepped.

Rebecca smoothed a large area and moved back to inspect her work, but her footprints immediately messed up the pattern that her cousin had just completed.

"Now you've stepped on my waves!" Ana complained.

Rebecca stopped working and looked over the pattern. "How can we make perfect waves when we're standing on them?" she asked. She shook her rake with frustration and then giggled. "Where's that soo-koo when you need it? Maybe we should just leave a very old rake behind and come back tomorrow. The soo-koo could groom the garden overnight—and it wouldn't leave any footprints!"

"Maybe only one person can work on this at a time," Ana said.

"It's sure a lot harder than I thought," Rebecca admitted, "but it's more fun if we do it together."

Just then, the bamboo door creaked open and a thin young man stepped through. Dark curls sprang helter-skelter from beneath his soft wool cap.

"What are you doing in here?" he demanded. "No visitors allowed."

"We're supposed to be here," Rebecca explained. "We're grooming the sand garden for Mr. Tanaka." She eyed the young man suspiciously. "What are *you* doing in here?"

He shrugged. "I heard you talking and came in to investigate. There's been some trouble in the garden lately, so I've been checking for trespassers."

Ana and Rebecca exchanged glances. "We heard about that this morning," Rebecca said.

"Every few days there's something more,"

the young man said. "And now that the garden construction has been completed, lots of workers have been let go, so there's hardly anyone left to make repairs except Mr. Tanaka."

"No wonder he needed helpers," Ana said. "Has it been happening all over the Botanic Garden?"

The young man scratched his head. "Now that you mention it, it's only happened in the Japanese Garden."

"How do we know *you're* not trespassing?" Rebecca asked.

"Well, aren't you filled with ginger," he said with a chuckle. "First of all, you can tell by my smock that I belong here." He tugged at a blue collar peeking out above his sweater, and Rebecca noticed that the fabric was exactly the same color as Mr. Tanaka's smock. The young man held out his hand, and each of the girls shook it politely. "I'm Nathaniel Gibney," he said. "I've been taking courses here since the Garden first opened. I volunteer here, too, because it's a great way to learn."

"I'm Rebecca, and this is my cousin Ana," Rebecca offered. "She wants to take the classes, too. She lives right here in Brooklyn."

"On Flatbush Avenue, to be exact," Ana said. "Do you live nearby?"

"Pretty close," Nathaniel mumbled. He sniffled and pulled a wrinkled handkerchief from his pocket to wipe his nose.

"We can't figure out how to make the wave pattern smooth," Ana confessed. "We keep stepping on each other's waves."

"It's pretty tricky," Nathaniel agreed. "Here's a hint: think what it would be like to paint a floor."

"Oh! It's like washing the kitchen floor!" Ana exclaimed. She poked Rebecca. "We just walk backward, as if we can't step on the wet tiles, and keep going until we're in the hall!"

"That's one way to look at it," Nathaniel said. "In fact, it's a swell idea."

"Now I've already learned something," Ana said, "and I've been here only an hour. We're going to be helping all week. Are you?"

"I'll be around," Nathaniel said over his shoulder, "keeping an eye on things." Then he slipped back out.

The girls returned to the raking, and Rebecca mulled over Nathaniel's words. Did he mean he was keeping an eye on them? Surely, he couldn't be suspicious of them, could he? The girls worked in silence, moving backward through the hidden garden. Birds trilled from the branches overhead.

"It does feel peaceful here, doesn't it?" said Ana, her voice barely louder than a whisper. She spread her arms wide, as if embracing the garden. "I'd like to be here every day for the rest of my life."

Once they reached the edge of the sand garden, the girls stood together, admiring their work. "We made a painting with sand," Ana said. "It's beautiful."

"It really is," Rebecca agreed. "But it took all morning. Let's go back to the plant house. Mr. Tanaka must be waiting for us."

A SECRET GARDEN

The girls linked arms and skipped all the way back to the plant house. Inside, they found Mr. Tanaka deftly pruning the bottom stalks from spotted yellow orchids. Their blossoms nodded at his touch, as if welcoming him. When he noticed Rebecca and Ana, he smiled but kept at his careful work.

Mrs. Tanaka came into the plant house and went directly into the storage room. She emerged a few moments later holding a bamboo basket. She watched her husband with admiration for a few moments before speaking to him in Japanese.

"Ah, yes, we should have lunch," he said. "I'm sure my young helpers worked up an appetite with their raking."

Ana slipped into the side room and soon returned with their lunch box. The girls joined the Tanakas at a table near where Miss Ward and her students were already eating.

Mrs. Tanaka had packed lunch in what

looked like a set of stacking baskets, and when she opened them, Rebecca saw that each basket contained a different food. Mrs. Tanaka spread the baskets on the table and then set four wooden sticks on a linen napkin. Rebecca watched in amazement as the gardener's wife balanced two of the polished sticks on her thumb and forefinger and deftly used them to pick up small rolls of rice and vegetables. She popped the rolls into her mouth expertly.

"Chopsticks," Mr. Tanaka said, noticing the girls' curious looks. He clicked the sticks close to their faces as if about to grab their noses. The girls pulled back and laughed.

"How do you do that?" Rebecca asked.

"We learn from the time we are small," Mr. Tanaka said, "so it is natural for us. When we first came to America, we couldn't figure out how to hold a fork in one hand and cut with a knife in the other. It felt so strange."

He picked up a ball of food with the chopsticks. "This doesn't need to be cut. It is already one perfect mouthful." He held it up for them to inspect. "These are made of carrots, cucumbers, and peppers wrapped in rice. My wife makes many different kinds, and they are always tasty." He smiled lovingly at Mrs. Tanaka, and Rebecca saw her blush. "Sometimes," the gardener said, "these *sushi* rolls have fish mixed in, too." He noticed the lunch the girls were sharing. "What is this round thing that you eat?"

"Oh, these are knishes," Ana said, holding one up. "It's a pastry with potato and onions stuffed inside."

"I guess knishes and sushi rolls aren't so different," Rebecca commented. "They're both little bites of lots of things rolled together." She added, "My aunt is going to teach us how to make them when we get home later. I can't wait!" She smiled at Mrs. Tanaka.

The gardener's wife almost smiled back, and Rebecca was glad to see that although Mrs. Tanaka might not be able to speak English well, she definitely seemed to understand it. *It would be nice if she smiled more*, Rebecca thought. *That works in any language.*

A GROWING SUSPICION

Rebecca wondered if the gardener's wife was often thinking of her son and feeling sad. She hoped Mrs. Tanaka wasn't unhappy about having her and Ana visiting the garden. She was so quiet, it was hard to tell.

The girls finished their lunches and stowed the lunch box in the storage room. By the time they returned, the others had cleared away their own meals and Mrs. Tanaka was already gone.

"What can we do now?" Ana asked eagerly.

"There are many chores to be attended to," Mr. Tanaka said, "but first, let me see how you completed your last job. Are the waves in the sand pond perfect?"

Ana's face lit up. "Once we figured out how to walk backward while we raked, it came out beautifully."

"Excellent," Mr. Tanaka said. "Let's have a look." They set off on the curving path that led from the plant house and turned off on the short path that led to the sand garden. Mr. Tanaka unlatched the door. The girls eagerly stepped inside, but then they stopped short. Instead of finding the space empty of visitors, Rebecca saw a well-dressed couple standing at the edge of the garden. They looked up, startled, when Mr. Tanaka entered.

What are they doing here? Rebecca wondered. She and Ana had left the door closed and latched. What was worse, she was dismayed to see footprints marring the perfect wave pattern that had taken so much time and care. Where was that Nathaniel fellow when there really *were* trespassers?

The two certainly weren't garden workers. The woman wore a flowered hat and had an elegant fur piece draped around her neck. The man looked dapper in a brushed derby hat. A gray silk ascot was tied at his neck, held neatly in place by a large pearl stickpin.

A concerned look creased Mr. Tanaka's forehead. He gave a deep bow, his hands pressed together. "A visit today is quite unexpected," he said. "This garden is not ready." Rebecca wondered why he was being so polite when clearly the pair had no business being there at all, much less trampling the carefully raked sand.

The elegantly dressed man barely acknowledged Mr. Tanaka and offered no apology. He walked off, tapping a silver-topped cane and guiding his companion right past the gardener and the girls as if they weren't even there. They walked arm in arm, the woman stepping carefully in her fashionable shoes.

Rebecca stared at their retreating backs. She couldn't understand why Mr. Tanaka had been so apologetic about asking them to leave. After all, they had entered an area that was clearly not open to the public. Nathaniel had been so quick to suspect her and Ana of trespassing when he found them working in the sand garden. Why wasn't Mr. Tanaka concerned about these two?

Yet the gardener seemed to instantly dismiss them from his thoughts. Instead, he focused on the sand garden. "You said you had worked diligently on the raking," he said with a note of disappointment, "but you have left footprints."

Rebecca didn't understand. He was blaming them for a problem they hadn't caused!

"It was perfect when we finished," Ana insisted. "Really, it was!"

"I think those visitors trampled right across the waves that we worked on so hard," Rebecca said.

"It is unkind to accuse others of one's own mistakes," Mr. Tanaka said gently. He walked to the edge of the garden and pointed to footprints left behind in a patch of damp sand. "Look. These footprints are small and light—like a child's."

Or like the footprints of a woman wearing fancy shoes, Rebecca thought. But she kept silent, worried that Mr. Tanaka would accuse her of blaming others again.

"I knew this was not a simple task," said Mr. Tanaka, not unkindly, "but I see that you still have much to learn." He shooed them out, closing the door firmly. "There is no more time to repair this today. I must tend to the ferns, as they are ready to be planted."

A Growing Suspicion

Mr. Tanaka's comments stung Rebecca's pride. Ana shuffled along morosely, her head down. Rebecca could guess exactly how her cousin felt. As they trudged back to the plant house, Rebecca felt increasingly annoyed at the fancy couple. *If the woman had tramped through the sand garden, what else might she have done? Could that couple be behind all the other problems that Nathaniel and Miss Ward had mentioned?*

4
MAKING A SPLASH

The girls followed Mr. Tanaka into the plant house, where a group of students was gathered around a large worktable covered with stacks of clay pots, shards of broken pottery, mounds of dark soil, and boxes of tiny seedlings. Miss Ward was directing their project.

When she saw the class, Ana perked up. She tugged at Rebecca's sleeve. "Let's listen for a minute," she said.

"These are lady ferns," Miss Ward was saying. "They need to be transplanted into larger pots. Place a few bits of broken clay in the bottom so that water can drain away from the roots. Then fill the pot halfway with soil, position the fern in the center, and fill the pot with soil around the plant. When we've potted these up,

43

we will mist the leaves with water. Ferns like moisture." She held up a glass bottle with a nozzle on top. Rebecca thought it looked a bit like a seltzer bottle in a candy shop. She couldn't help thinking of foamy egg creams.

After watching for a moment, Rebecca turned to hurry after Mr. Tanaka, but she realized that Ana was still listening to Miss Ward. "Come on, Ana," Rebecca said gently. "We can't stay."

"I wish I could," Ana said as Miss Ward's voice faded into the distance. "If I learn enough, I might be able to come back this summer."

As they approached the bench where Mr. Tanaka waited for them, they could see that he, too, was caring for ferns. He was spraying large potted ferns with the same type of bottle Miss Ward had used.

"I can do that for you," Ana offered.

"Good," said Mr. Tanaka, handing her the mister. "You will make a fine gardener yet."

"These leaves look like lacy green doilies," Ana commented. "I'd give anything to have some ferns like this in my own garden." She finished misting the plants and turned back to Mr. Tanaka. "Can we pot up some of the smaller ferns now, like the students?"

"It is time for us to stop for the day," said Mr. Tanaka. "Tomorrow we can work again with ferns—if you would like to come back, of course."

"Oh, yes," Ana said.

Rebecca was growing tired of her day at the Botanic Garden and was a bit relieved to learn they would soon head home. Maybe there would still be enough time to make knishes with Aunt Fannie. The thought gave her spirits a lift.

When they got off the trolley near the apartment, the girls thanked the Tanakas for their wonderful day, and then Rebecca dashed ahead.

"I'll race you up the steps," she shouted to Ana. Rebecca took the stairs two at a time. She reached the top, out of breath, with Ana just a step behind her.

"Knishes!" they shouted as they burst into the kitchen.

Aunt Fannie was at the sink, washing

potatoes. "So, it was a good day at these gardens?" she asked. "And still you are ready to cook?"

Rebecca snapped to attention and gave a little salute, and Ana stepped up beside her and did the same. "Reporting for kitchen duty," Rebecca said.

"Then you are the ones peeling and cutting potatoes," Aunt Fannie said. "That is first step of making knishes. Today we will cook all the potatoes, and tomorrow, we roll and bake. First," she said, checking Ana's hands, "get rid of garden dirt!"

The girls washed in the bathroom sink, splashing water at each other as they did. "I am not a fern," Ana declared with a giggle, "so stop *spritzing* me!"

Together, the girls began paring potatoes in the kitchen. "I liked visiting the garden," said Rebecca, dropping a peeled potato into the pot, "but learning to cook is going to be even better. At least no one can mess up our knishes!"

Making a Splash

The next morning at the garden, Mr. Tanaka set to work the moment he entered the glass plant house. Mrs. Tanaka took the lunch box from Ana and headed to the side room to store it along with her own. Rebecca and Ana waited beside Mr. Tanaka at a workbench as he counted pots of lacy ferns lined up in rows.

"Today we work on the fern garden," he announced. "Help me load up the larger ferns, and I'll show you how to plant them."

The girls placed the potted plants in a wheelbarrow with care. The wooden wheel at the front rumbled as Mr. Tanaka pushed the cart along the stony path.

He stopped at a hillside facing the edge of the pond. An alcove had been carved into the side of the hill. Inside it were flat tiers of soil that formed steps from the bottom to the top. Mr. Tanaka pulled two sharp-pointed hand trowels from the wheelbarrow and laid them on the ground.

"For this job, you must arrange eight plants on each level," he explained. "Dig each hole bigger than the fern, and loosen the soil. Then tap the plant from the pot like this." He tipped a pot and gently rapped the bottom and sides with the handle of a trowel until the fern slid out, soil still clinging to its roots. "Next, set the plant in the hole and add soil to the top of the roots—like this." He knelt on the bare dirt and demonstrated. "Make sure each fern is standing straight." He looked at the girls a bit uncertainly. "I'm sure you will do better today than yesterday."

"But Mr. Tanaka, we . . ." Rebecca began to protest, but she fell silent when Ana flashed her a warning look. Ana was probably right to silence her, Rebecca thought. She didn't want to argue with the gardener, even if he had misjudged them. Instead, they would have to do a perfect job and make sure their work stayed undisturbed.

"Let's dig all the holes first," Ana suggested, "and then plant the ferns." She stepped to the top of the alcove, balancing carefully. "I'll start up here, and you start at the bottom."

Rebecca began digging in the packed dirt with her trowel. Every scoop hit small stones that had to be picked out and tossed away. It was tedious work. Rebecca tried to pass the time by imagining herself in a movie as the gardener's lovely wife, but she soon grew bored. A loud splash from the pond distracted her. She walked to the water's edge and peered down. A flash of color swished beneath the surface.

"What beautiful fish!" she exclaimed.

Ana clambered down and stood beside her. Fat fish skimmed along, pushing their mouths up over the water. Some were bright orange with patches that gleamed silvery white, and others were vivid black and red.

"Except for the colors, these remind me of the carp that Mama kept in a washtub right before Passover," Ana said. "Mama wanted her *gefilte fish* to be perfectly fresh. I wanted to keep them as pets. I just couldn't bear to think of them being cooked into fish cakes!"

A Growing Suspicion

Rebecca shuddered at the idea of turning these painted pond fish into dinner.

"Well, we've got a lot of work to do," Ana said, nudging Rebecca. "I want Mr. Tanaka to see how *responsible* I am. We didn't get off to a very good start yesterday."

The girls returned to their digging, but Rebecca's heart wasn't in the task. She couldn't stop thinking about how disappointed Mr. Tanaka had been with the sand garden. She didn't like being blamed unfairly.

"Let's go back to the secret garden and check around," she suggested. "We have to prove that we didn't leave those footprints."

Ana kept working. "Maybe after we plant the ferns," she said.

The cousins dug one hole after another until Rebecca's muscles ached. She stood up and rubbed her stiff neck. "Look," she said, pointing across the pond. "There's the couple that was in the sand garden yesterday."

Ana climbed down again, and the girls peered at two people on a small island, leaning against some low boulders.

"I'm sure it's them," Rebecca declared. "No one else here wears such fancy clothes. How did they get out there?"

The woman gestured toward some shrubs, and then Rebecca distinctly saw her pluck a blossom and tuck it into the man's lapel before they walked on.

"She picked a flower!" Rebecca fumed. "Miss Ward told us not to take even a dead leaf! Those two act as if they own the place, but I'll bet they're up to no good. I think we should find out what's going on."

"We'd better not," Ana protested. "We promised . . ." But Rebecca strode down the path that wound around the pond, pulling Ana along.

"Let's keep working," Ana said, trying to turn back. "The holes are almost done, and we can plant the ferns lickety-split."

"This could be our only chance to investigate," Rebecca said. "If they left footprints behind, we can go back to the sand garden and see if they match. Then we'd know they were the ones who messed it up."

She held Ana's hand firmly and circled around the pond. As she walked farther along the path bordering the bank, something else drew her attention. "Look at those birds!" she said, pointing to two long-legged birds wading next to the tiny island in the pond. "I didn't notice them before. Do you think they're real?" One of the birds bent its neck to the water, as if hunting for fish. The second bird stretched its long neck to the sky.

"We really have to get back to the fern garden," Ana said, pulling her hand free, "before you get us into hot water." She tapped a bamboo railing that blocked the bank leading from the pathway to the pond. "Anyway, there's no way down."

"That couple got down there somehow," Rebecca mused. She walked a bit farther, looking for an opening in the low fence. "There!" She pointed to a steep path that led to a bridge. The narrow bamboo bridge arched over a stream that separated the main garden from the tiny island. Without hesitating, Rebecca tripped down the path and carefully crossed the bridge.

Rebecca stepped onto the island and began searching the ground for footprints. Instead of a sandy bank, smooth stones and pebbles rolled under her feet. The bank was too stony for footprints.

"Come back," Ana called down to her. "Please, Beckie!"

Rebecca waved gaily to her cousin and moved closer to the island's edge, hoping to find soft sand there. Instead, she discovered a curving line of large round stepping-stones that led across the water and toward the unmoving birds. They were made of bronze, yet they seemed so lifelike, she almost expected them to fly away. Everything was so intriguing that all thoughts of finding clues about the mysterious couple disappeared from Rebecca's head.

"Watch this, Ana," she shouted as she hopped onto the first stone. "I'm dancing across the water!"

A Growing Suspicion

Rebecca swept her arms in graceful arcs, imagining that she was dressed in a silk kimono with flowing sleeves. She was starring in *The Gardener's Wife* again, with the cameraman turning the handle on his movie camera. She did a pirouette on the flat stone, feeling it wobble slightly as she twirled. She pretended to take mincing steps in embroidered slippers as she skipped onto the next stone. She reached out to stroke the bird statue nearby and then pressed her palms together and bowed, imitating Mr. Tanaka. She glanced up and saw Ana smile.

Feeling encouraged, Rebecca danced from one stone to the next, farther and farther from shore. She picked a fallen leaf from the water and waved it in front of her face like a fan. Ana began to laugh at Rebecca's antics. Then, in the midst of a one-legged spin, her arms outstretched, Rebecca was startled by a shout from the bridge above her.

"Come up here at once, young lady!" a voice called sharply.

MAKING A SPLASH

Miss Ward and her class appeared on the wide wooden bridge high above the pond. Nathaniel was right beside the teacher. Her face darkened.

Rebecca's vision of the Japanese dance burst like a soap bubble. She jumped back across the stones in a panic. Miss Ward would be furious—and worse, Ana would be, too.

Just as Rebecca landed with two feet on the stepping-stone closest to shore, it teetered, throwing her off balance. Rebecca stumbled into the pond with a splash.

5
UGLY SUSPICIONS

Cold water sloshed up to Rebecca's knees.
The shock sent her scrambling awkwardly back
onto the bank. The hem of her dress was soaked,
her stockings sagged, and water squished from
her shoes. What would Papa say if she had
ruined her shoes?

Rebecca saw Miss Ward pull Nathaniel aside
and tell him something. Then she watched him
dash off toward the plant house, his blue smock
flapping against his back. He must be going to
get Mr. Tanaka!

The arched bridge at the opposite end of
the island had led Rebecca across, but now it
seemed too far away to reach quickly. With Miss
Ward glaring at her and the students snickering,
she decided that the fastest way back to the path

was to clamber up the embankment.

Rebecca scrambled straight up the steep bank. When she reached the fence, she pulled off her shoes and poured out the water that had filled them. Holding her shoes in one hand, she tried to climb over the railing. Just as she lifted one leg over the fence, her wet stocking slid on the slippery grass and she fell forward. There was a sickening crunch as the bamboo fence broke beneath her. Miss Ward's students let out a loud gasp.

Rebecca's knees shook as she stood up and looked dismally at the splintered fence. Mr. Tanaka appeared at her side like a pale apparition, shaking his head at the sight of the shattered railings. "So you have left the task I gave you," he said. "Now there is one more thing that must be repaired."

Rebecca's face flushed. "I—I know I shouldn't have gone down to the island," she admitted, "but I was trying to find out what the fancy couple was doing down there. I wouldn't have fallen into the pond if the stone hadn't tipped!"

Miss Ward hurried toward them. Rebecca braced herself for the anger that would surely pour down like another splash of cold water, but Miss Ward simply scowled at her. The silence felt more frightening than anything the teacher might say.

Mr. Tanaka walked across the bridge to the island's edge and began testing the stepping-stone with both hands. It slid off a cement post hidden just beneath the surface of the water and toppled onto its side. Mr. Tanaka lifted the stone from the shallow water onto the pebbled shore and then walked back to the path where Rebecca stood, dripping.

"I thought the stone was properly anchored to the post," he said, "but the cement is cracked right through. Thank goodness no visitors stepped on the stone and fell in. That would have been far worse."

Now Rebecca was indignant. Was Mr. Tanaka saying that it was better for her to fall into the pond instead of the fancy-dressed couple? Perhaps Rebecca shouldn't have strayed onto the island when she was supposed to be planting ferns, but at least she hadn't picked a precious flower!

Miss Ward looked anxiously at the gardener. "Can you repair it?"

"I can cement it back onto the post," said Mr. Tanaka, "but it is going to take time. The post must be removed and dried. Then the stone must be cemented on. Finally, it must be set properly back in the water."

Miss Ward frowned and turned her attention to the damaged fence. "Nathaniel can get some wood and nail this back together."

"No, no," Mr. Tanaka interrupted. "In a traditional Japanese garden, fences are tied carefully with raffia twine, not built with nails. I will cut new bamboo rails and repair it just so."

Rebecca stole a glance at her cousin, who stood with her arms folded and her face red. She couldn't meet Ana's eyes. Rebecca had promised her parents that she wouldn't cause Aunt Fannie or Uncle Jacob any trouble during her visit. Now she had caused more trouble than she could have imagined—for Ana.

"I will remove the post today and let it dry overnight," Mr. Tanaka said. He surveyed the area. "This part of the path must be closed. No visitors until everything is safe."

"So many things going wrong," murmured Miss Ward, "and just when we need everything to be in perfect order." She clamped her mouth into a tight line and finally addressed Rebecca. "If you cannot obey the rules, you and your cousin will not be welcome here."

"Oh, please, Miss Ward," Ana begged. "It wasn't *my* fault! *I* didn't go onto the island." She glared at Rebecca.

"My young helpers should not have come here alone," Mr. Tanaka said, "but the loose stone would have caused an accident sometime, even if not today. And the fence is an unfortunate event, but an accident—not like the other problems." He barely paused before adding, "The fault is mine for leaving these girls unsupervised."

Rebecca's stomach clenched. She might have ruined Ana's chances of spending the week in a place she loved, and now poor Mr. Tanaka was taking the blame. She hung her head.

Nathaniel stifled a cough. "It's one mess after another," he muttered dismally. His expression became more sympathetic when he looked at Rebecca, shivering in her wet clothes. He took off his blue smock, revealing a wrinkled shirt, and draped the smock over Rebecca's shoulders. The soft cotton felt warm against her back.

"Oh, no," she protested. "I couldn't take this when you need it yourself. You already have a cold." She tried to hand the smock back, but Nathaniel refused.

"Go back to the plant house immediately," Miss Ward ordered Rebecca. "You might as well be in a warm place while we discuss this situation." She walked back toward her class. "I will join you there directly."

Her teeth chattering, Rebecca hurried on ahead. She thought Ana would join her, but she realized that her cousin was keeping as far away as she could. *She doesn't even want to be near me,* Rebecca thought.

Across the pond, a flash of lavender disappeared behind a willow tree, its yellow-green leaves forming a curtain that nearly touched the ground. The sight made Rebecca feel even worse. *Mrs. Tanaka must have seen everything that happened. Now there is one more person who will be angry,* she thought. *I've made a mess of everything!*

Rebecca's feet felt numb, and it was difficult to walk without her shoes, but she fairly ran the last several yards toward the beckoning greenhouse. As she approached, the glass door swung open, and Rebecca was stunned to see the well-dressed woman hurrying out. She held a tall, cloth-draped object partly covered by her open coat. What was she hiding?

Rebecca stared as the woman tottered along the gravel path in her high-heeled shoes. A light gust of wind lifted the edge of the cloth, giving Rebecca a glimpse of a glazed green pot and a hint of spotted yellow blossoms. It was one of the orchids Mr. Tanaka had been pruning. The woman was carrying off one of his plants!

Nathaniel came running up with a pair of woolen socks and ushered Rebecca inside as the others joined them. Rebecca pulled off her soggy stockings and put on Nathaniel's dry socks, but neither the thick socks nor the heat inside the plant house were enough to warm her. She watched Ana standing stiffly apart and felt a different kind of chill.

When Miss Ward entered, Rebecca was still shivering. "You really must take these children home at once," Miss Ward said to Mr. Tanaka. She fidgeted with her clipboard. "I'm sorry you are going to lose the rest of the day, but it can't be avoided."

Mr. Tanaka looked pained. "Please accept my apologies for so much difficulty." He bowed his head. "I will inform Mr. Gager about the damage. I know he will be concerned to hear about it."

Miss Ward let out a deep sigh. "He certainly will," she agreed. "The damage to the fence and the stepping-stone couldn't have come at a worse time."

Rebecca noticed Mrs. Tanaka standing at the door, ready to leave, the handle of her lunch basket over her arm. Rebecca hadn't heard her come in. "Do not forget lunch," Mrs. Tanaka murmured.

"We haven't even been here long enough to eat," said Ana. "My lunch box is still in the side room."

"I'll get it," Nathaniel volunteered, dashing off while the group stood in awkward silence. He returned with the lunch box tucked under his arm.

As Ana lifted the box from Nathaniel's arms, the lid fell open. Out tumbled their lunch—and something small and heavy that landed with a crash.

"Oh!" gasped Rebecca. There on the tile floor, along with two bagels Aunt Fannie had packed, were shards of clay pottery, clumps of soil, and the crushed remains of a tiny lady fern. Rebecca stared helplessly at the mess on the floor, while Ana backed away.

Miss Ward picked up a piece of the shattered pot and held it out like evidence in a trial. "To think that Mr. Tanaka allowed you girls to spend time here and this is how you repay his kindness!"

"I never touched the ferns!" Ana cried.

"Neither did I!" Rebecca insisted, facing her cousin with dismay. "I wasn't even in the storage area. Someone else must have put it there! And look," she said, pointing to the clasp on the lunchbox. "The buckle was undone." Rebecca was shocked by Ana's doubtful look. Could her cousin really think she would do such a thing?

Ana's lower lip quivered as she turned to Miss Ward. "Does this mean I can't take classes in the summer?"

"I don't see how that would be possible after all that has transpired," Miss Ward replied. "It's clear that you are not ready for such responsibility."

Ana looked miserable. As Rebecca looked at her cousin, a terrible thought crept into her mind. Ana had said she would give anything to have a fern. Had she found a moment to visit the storeroom and slip one into her box? Had she wanted a fern for her new garden so badly that she would take one?

As soon as the idea entered her head, Rebecca dismissed it instantly, ashamed of herself for even thinking such a thing. Ana would never steal a plant—no matter how much she longed for one. Surely Ana must know that Rebecca wouldn't steal anything, either.

Rebecca put her hand on her cousin's arm to comfort her, but Ana pulled away. Rebecca's heart sank. She had never meant to ruin Ana's best chance to spend time at the Botanic Garden, but she had. She had also spoiled all the fun of spending the week together. Ana probably wouldn't even want to talk to her now.

"It would be completely unfair to keep Ana away," Rebecca protested, trying to repair the blow to her cousin's reputation. "Please don't punish her for things that were my fault."

Miss Ward seemed unmoved. She pointed

to the crushed plant lying with the soil and pottery shards. "What can you say to excuse that?" she demanded.

Rebecca sputtered, unsure what to say. Her thoughts were in a jumble. Was someone trying to get both her and Ana into trouble? Could someone have put the fern in their lunch box and left the clasp undone so that the plant would fall out in front of everyone at lunch? She went over the incident in her mind. Nathaniel had brought the box from the storeroom just now. If he had slipped the fern inside, no one would have seen him. This morning when they'd first arrived at the plant house, Mrs. Tanaka had put their lunch away. She had been alone with it in the storeroom, too.

Rebecca shook her head, trying to clear it of such ugly suspicions, just as she had pushed out the thought of Ana taking the fern. Nathaniel had no reason to do such a mean thing. In fact, so far, he had been helpful and kind. Mrs. Tanaka had not been very friendly, but that could be explained by the loss of her son.

A GROWING SUSPICION

Rebecca couldn't even bring herself to blame the well-dressed lady. She had been alone in the plant house, too, and she *had* been hiding a plant under her coat, but how could she have known that the lunch box belonged to the girls?

One look at Ana's sorrowful face and Miss Ward's angry one made Rebecca want to blame someone, but truly, no one had any reason to put her and Ana into such a terrible fix. Seeing Ana fighting back tears, Rebecca swallowed hard to keep herself from crying.

After a silence that seemed to last forever, Mr. Tanaka spoke. In a soft voice he said, "Things have been going wrong in the Japanese Garden for weeks, so the girls may not be at fault. They say they are innocent, and I believe them. They have done their best to help me. Since so many workers have been let go, I need extra hands more than ever."

Miss Ward's face softened slightly. She looked from Ana to Rebecca. "If Mr. Tanaka sees fit to allow you back in the garden, I will not stand in the way. Be warned, however. If there are any further incidents, I will see to it that you are barred from returning, and I will personally inform your parents of the damage you have caused."

Rebecca caught her breath. If that happened, Mama would surely make Rebecca return home immediately. She'd never get the chance to learn how to make Aunt Fannie's knishes. In fact, she might not be allowed to visit Ana on her own again.

Mr. Tanaka pointed to a gnarly tree whose limbs stretched out to one side as if reaching for something. "Do you see how sturdy and graceful this tree is?" he asked. "I trained it by trimming off branches that were not desirable and guiding the others in the best direction. This is how young people must be trained as they grow." He looked kindly at the girls. "You must trim away the habits that are undesirable and help the honorable ones to grow stronger. You have a chance to repair your reputations here, but you must be willing to work care-fully." The girls nodded their agreement, and

A Growing Suspicion

Mr. Tanaka addressed Miss Ward. "We will come early tomorrow and get to work."

Ana wiped away the tears that were now spilling down her cheeks. "Please don't cry," Rebecca said. "At least we can come back with Mr. Tanaka. Maybe we can find a way to make things right."

"I know *I* can," Ana said, "but you only seem to know how to make things go wrong!"

Tears stung Rebecca's eyes. Mr. Tanaka might have forgiven her for what had happened today, but would Ana?

The only way to fix things would be to prove that neither of them had taken the fern. But how?

6
ANOTHER SUSPICIOUS EVENT

"Home so soon?" Aunt Fannie asked when the girls returned. "Now we have plenty of time to bake knishes." Her smile turned to a frown when she saw Rebecca's wet clothes.

"What has happened? You are swimming on such a cold day?" she joked. Rebecca could see that she was trying to hide her concern.

Before Rebecca could utter a word, Ana covered for her. "Poor Beckie slipped at the edge of the pond," she said coolly, "and got a little wet."

Ana's excuse was true—as far as it went—and Rebecca was heartened that her cousin hadn't tattled on her. Maybe Ana wasn't as angry with her now that Miss Ward had agreed to let them return tomorrow. Or had Ana kept

the full story from Aunt Fannie only because
she didn't want to hurt her own chances of
going back to the Japanese Garden?

"I'm sorry for all the trouble," Rebecca said.
"I'll wash these clothes myself, Aunt Fannie.
I don't want to make more work for you."

"Nothing to worry about," her aunt said.
"Now, quick you get into nice hot bath, then
put on dry clothes."

Rebecca soaked in the luxurious bathtub,
dreaming what it would be like to have one in
her family's apartment. She could take a bath
every day, not just on Friday afternoon in
a washtub set up in the middle of the kitchen.

By the time she was dried and dressed in
fresh clothes, Aunt Fannie had set out bowls
on the kitchen table with yesterday's cooked
potatoes, and fresh onions and mushrooms.
Rebecca tried to ignore the pile of wet clothes
on the floor under the sink and her wet shoes
nestled under the warm stove.

"Come, Ana!" Aunt Fannie called.

Ana appeared at the kitchen doorway, an

open book in her hand. "I'm at a really exciting part of my book," she said, but Rebecca heard the falseness in her voice. "You two make the knishes. I can learn some other time."

Rebecca followed her cousin to her bedroom door. "It's not fun unless we make them together," she protested.

"Not today," Ana said with finality. Then she closed her bedroom door.

Rebecca could barely pay attention as Aunt Fannie showed her how to cook the chopped onions and mushrooms in a frying pan until they were soft and fragrant, and then mix them with the potatoes.

Aunt Fannie explained how many eggs and how much flour to mix with the potatoes for the dough, but seconds later, Rebecca couldn't remember. She rolled the dough out mechanically, cut it into squares, and plopped in the filling. Aunt Fannie showed her how to pinch the edges of the dough together and hide the fold at the bottom so that the knishes would bake with perfectly rounded tops.

A GROWING SUSPICION

"Now the secret to make them shiny on top," Aunt Fannie said when the knishes were lined up on baking sheets. She cracked an egg into a small bowl, added a few drops of water, and mixed it with a fork.

"Dip fingers into egg and rub gently across tops," she said. Rebecca dipped her fingertips into the egg mixture. *This should be the most fun part of the recipe,* she thought, *but without Ana it isn't at all.*

At dinner, Ana barely spoke. Aunt Fannie shared the fresh knishes with the family and announced that they were "Beckie baked!" Ana still ignored her, and Rebecca felt none of the joy she had expected after learning to make a treat she had always loved. The knishes didn't even taste the way she remembered.

She said good night early, but when she walked into the bedroom, the room was dark, and Ana's face was turned to the wall.

"Ana," Rebecca whispered, "don't be angry." Was Ana asleep—or just pretending to be? Rebecca crawled into bed and blinked back tears. How could she make things better tomorrow? There had to be a way.

At breakfast, Ana was still barely speaking to Rebecca. "I'll make up for everything today," Rebecca promised. "I'll be the perfect helper." Ana ignored her.

Aunt Fannie had done all the laundering, including Rebecca's dress, Nathaniel's smock, and his thick socks.

"They are still hanging in bathroom," Aunt Fannie said with a smile. "Not dry yet. Please tell your friend you bring his things tomorrow."

Rebecca felt a wave of gratitude for Aunt Fannie's kindness. "Thank you for doing that," she said and hugged her aunt warmly. When Aunt Fannie put her arms around her, Rebecca nearly burst into tears. Yesterday had been the worst day. Rebecca could barely think about how she would manage to spend another day at the Japanese Garden, but she knew that if she declined to go, Aunt Fanny would make Ana stay home, too.

She checked her shoes and was relieved to discover that although they were stiff and needed a fresh coat of polish, they had dried overnight under the warm kitchen stove. In the bathroom, she felt the damp clothes hanging above the sink. She wondered where Nathaniel had gotten the socks. It seemed odd that he had had an extra pair with him.

As Rebecca turned to leave, something shiny near the sink drain caught her eye. She picked up a small brass key. *Lucky it didn't wash down the drain,* Rebecca thought. Guessing that someone in the family had forgotten it, she set it safely on the ledge of the tub, where it would be easily found. Then she walked to the door and tried to stand taller. She would get to the bottom of whatever was going on at the Japanese Garden and make things right with Ana again. She had to.

The girls met the Tanakas in front of the building and waited for the trolley in silence.

ANOTHER SUSPICIOUS EVENT

Besides worrying about how to make things up to Ana, Rebecca felt guilty to have the gardener paying for carfare. So far she had paid him back with problems.

Mrs. Tanaka spoke rapidly in Japanese to her husband, her tone impatient. Mr. Tanaka stroked her hand soothingly and answered calmly yet firmly. Rebecca didn't know what they were discussing, but she guessed it was about her and Ana. As they climbed aboard the trolley, Mrs. Tanaka leaned close to Rebecca's ear and said quietly, "No more trouble today."

Rebecca's face flushed with embarrassment. Today she would do whatever Mr. Tanaka asked, and do it perfectly. She also had to find a way to prove that both she and Ana were innocent of all the mishaps. The problem was, she had no idea where to begin.

When they arrived at the plant house, Mrs. Tanaka snipped some flowers for her daily arrangement. She chose two slender leafy stalks and two orchid stems and headed off to the teahouse, gliding past the girls as if they weren't even there. Rebecca felt that Mrs. Tanaka was scolding them with her silence.

Mr. Tanaka handed Rebecca a hammer and gave Ana a thick roll of raffia. He slung a canvas bag filled with golden yellow bamboo rods across his back. Rebecca and Ana followed him over the wooden bridge—the same bridge where Miss Ward and her class had stood when Rebecca had splashed into the pond. Today Rebecca saw how perfectly the landscape blended together. On the left, a triple waterfall cascaded over rocks and tumbled into a rushing brook. It swirled beneath the bridge and flowed into the pond.

Looking down, Rebecca cringed at the sight of the splintered fence and the missing stepping-stone. The pillar and stone had been left to dry on the path, and the entire walkway was blocked off with heavy rope. Rebecca couldn't bear to think of how she had damaged the beautiful view.

She and Ana crossed the bridge with Mr. Tanaka. They passed the ridge where Rebecca had seen the tall stone lantern, but today there was no sign of it. Instead, as they drew closer, they nearly bumped into Nathaniel. Beside him, Miss Ward stood with a middle-aged man in a dark suit and topcoat. They all looked grim.

At Nathaniel's feet, sections of the stone lantern were strewn in a ragged pile. The stately sculpture had toppled to the ground, crushing the ferns that surrounded it.

"I found it lying across the path," Nathaniel explained to Miss Ward.

The teacher turned to Ana and Rebecca. "Why is it that every time something has gone wrong in the past two days, you two have not been far away?"

That was so unfair! How could Miss Ward accuse them of a misdeed just because they were standing nearby? After all, Mr. Tanaka and

Nathaniel had both come upon the toppled lantern, and they weren't accused of being involved.

Rebecca had promised herself to stay clear of trouble, and already she was being reprimanded—when she hadn't done anything!

She studied the gentleman with Miss Ward. He wore a spiffy derby hat similar to the one the mysterious man in the sand garden had worn, but he wasn't dressed as lavishly and carried no cane. Rebecca guessed he must be the director of the Botanic Garden.

"I'm afraid we have more damage, Mr. Gager," the teacher said. The director watched as Mr. Tanaka shook his head sadly over the crushed plants.

"I am not pleased to meet you young ladies under such circumstances," said Mr. Gager. Rebecca could barely look him in the face. He must have heard about Rebecca's accident and the fern plant that had fallen from their lunch box.

"I don't believe they caused this, sir."

Nathaniel's voice sounded confident. "It happened before they arrived this morning."

Rebecca felt a flurry of relief. Miss Ward and Mr. Gager seemed quite willing to believe Nathaniel.

"Anyone could have been in this area," the director mused, rubbing his chin thoughtfully. "It's a popular path. Perhaps some unruly visitors pushed the lantern over, thinking it was just a lark." He clucked his disapproval.

"Before I left last night," said Miss Ward, "I took a brisk walk around, and the lantern was standing tall. Someone must have done this after closing time—or quite early this morning. Who would be here after hours?"

Rebecca thought first of Nathaniel, who always seemed to be around. She puzzled over what she knew about him. He often seemed to be wandering on his own, just as when he came into the sand garden on her first day. Something about Nathaniel's presence didn't seem quite right.

She thought also of the suspicious couple

who had entered the hidden sand garden. The woman had picked a flower at the island, and Rebecca had seen her later, sneaking out of the plant house hiding an orchid. Could the pair have found a way to get into the Japanese Garden and toppled the lantern? What Rebecca had seen might be an important clue. She had to let the director know.

"The day before yesterday," Rebecca began, "there was a man and a woman in the sand garden." She turned to Mr. Tanaka. "Remember?" she asked. "And then yesterday, when I was going to the greenhouse, I saw the very same woman sneaking out with an orchid hidden under her coat!"

Rebecca expected the director to take a keen interest in this news. Instead, he dismissed her with a curt wave of his hand. "Don't try to blame this on visitors," he said. "I'd advise you to tend to your own tasks and not concern yourself with what others are doing."

Rebecca looked at the director in disbelief. Why didn't he take her information seriously?

Hadn't he himself suggested that visitors might have knocked over the lantern as a lark?

Mr. Tanaka examined the lantern sections that lay scattered on the ground. "Thankfully, each piece is undamaged," he announced, "and each is meant to be stacked on the next like a tower." He pushed his glasses up on his nose. "I'll need some help to lift the sections, but the lantern can be repaired. Even the ferns can be replaced today."

Nathaniel leaned down and tried to lift one of the lantern pieces, grunting. "If you lift one end," he said to Mr. Tanaka, "we can fix this. I'll come back as soon as the class has a break."

"I'm afraid there are no other workers to spare," the director told Mr. Tanaka. "As you know, we've had to reduce our staff." He cleared his throat. "Of course, we couldn't have guessed there would suddenly be so much damage."

Mr. Tanaka looked pained. "Perhaps Nathaniel can be of assistance," he murmured.

"I'm confident you will see to things," said Mr. Gager. With that, he strode away.

A Growing Suspicion

Nathaniel followed Miss Ward, and Rebecca heard his deep cough echoing behind her. She noted with concern that Nathaniel wasn't wearing a smock today. His shirt and pants were quite rumpled, and he had no jacket. He must have lent her his only smock. She had neglected to tell him that it was not yet dry.

"I am going to be *quite* busy here," Mr. Tanaka told the girls, "and I think you should stay out of Miss Ward's way. Leave the tools with me, and go visit my wife at the teahouse. You may observe as she designs the ikebana. Once Miss Ward is occupied with her students, I will have you come and assist me with other projects." He pointed toward a wooded path, and Ana and Rebecca headed off together.

Rebecca was cheered by the prospect of visiting the teahouse, and she could see that Ana's spirits had lifted, too. "At last we'll have a chance to see the flower arranging," Ana said.

"That's true," Rebecca agreed, relieved that at least Ana had spoken to her. "But I don't think Mrs. Tanaka is going to be very pleased to see us.

ANOTHER SUSPICIOUS EVENT

Maybe she thinks we really are causing all the problems here."

Now that Ana was listening to her, Rebecca tried again to persuade her not to be angry. "I know we can find out what's going on," she added, "and who's responsible—but we have to work together!"

Ana let out a deep breath. "Please, Beckie," she said, "promise me that you'll do what Mr. Tanaka says. If he and Miss Ward haven't been able to solve the mystery, we're not going to, either. It's just going to cause more trouble if we try." She paused and then added, "Though I suppose it can't hurt just to talk about it. I've been thinking about all that's happened, and I do feel Nathaniel is acting mighty suspiciously. He was the first one to discover the broken lantern. How do we know that he didn't push it over?"

"Well, he's helped us a lot," Rebecca observed, "and he spoke up for us just now. But he is always showing up at odd times, and he's usually alone. It sure does seem as if he's close by whenever something goes wrong."

"I know," Ana agreed. "He came in when we were working on the sand garden. He could have made the footprints after we left."

"And he was the one who brought the lunch box just before the fern fell out," Rebecca said. At that, Ana was quiet again, and Rebecca worried that her cousin still suspected her. "Until we know who else might have done those things," Rebecca said, "we should keep an eye on Nathaniel." She wasn't sure that Ana agreed with her. *At least,* Rebecca thought hopefully, *she didn't disagree.*

The girls came to a fork in the path. One way continued around the pond, and the other offered stone steps that led to a steep path.

"Which way?" Ana asked.

Just then, Rebecca heard voices arguing. She pulled Ana behind a stand of large rocks and raised her finger to her lips. "Listen," she whispered.

Rebecca heard Nathaniel's voice rising and a second voice speaking softly. She couldn't tell whom he was talking with, but it sounded like a woman.

"Please don't," Nathaniel begged. "Please! I don't have any other choice." There was a muffled answer that Rebecca couldn't make out. Then Nathaniel spoke again. "No," he insisted. "I won't!"

The voices faded away, and Rebecca and Ana looked at each other in confusion. Rebecca heard the crunch of gravel under receding footsteps, followed by silence. The girls stepped cautiously from behind the rocks. There was no one in sight.

"I wonder who was with Nathaniel," Ana said. "It sure sounded as though he did something wrong."

"Let's keep going and see if we can learn anything new," said Rebecca.

They moved a short distance along the path and came to a clearing where a small structure stood behind a picket fence. Dark pines rose behind it.

"I wonder if that's the teahouse," Rebecca

said. The raised building had a sloping roofline with edges that curled up at the four corners. Swirling designs were carved into the wood and highlighted in white paint.

Suddenly Ana froze. "Look at those!" she said under her breath.

Two lifelike statues of gray foxes stood guard at the entrance gate. "It's as if they're staring at us," Rebecca said.

"I think they're a warning to stay away," Ana said, still not moving. "One of them is snarling. They almost look real enough to bite!"

"They are a bit creepy," Rebecca admitted, "but they're only statues." She stepped cautiously between the two foxes and approached the gate. A rusty padlock was looped through the latch. Rebecca gave it a tug. It was securely fastened, just like the one at the toolshed in Ana's backyard. "Nathaniel and whoever he was arguing with must have been right near here," she said. "Maybe there's another way to get in."

"Don't you dare try!" Ana warned. "This is not the teahouse, or Mrs. Tanaka would be here.

And the gate is locked, so this must be closed to visitors. You've gotten us into enough trouble already, Rebecca Rubin, and I'm not going to let you cause any more. I'm leaving to find the teahouse, whether you come with me or not."

With that, Ana stalked off, leaving Rebecca looking with determination at the mysterious building.

7
A DISCOVERY IN THE WOODS

Rebecca heard the blame in Ana's words. She knew she should follow her cousin to the teahouse, but the tiny structure might hold some clue about who—or what—was behind all the strange happenings.

I just have to take a peek inside, Rebecca thought. She skirted the fenced area surrounding the building. *Maybe there's a window and I can see what's inside.* But every wall was made of solid wood panels.

Rebecca rolled a large stone against the picket fence and used it as a step to climb over the top. *Now,* she thought keenly, *let's see what's inside this little building.*

She tiptoed up the steep wooden steps at the front and faced two paneled doors. She felt a flutter in her chest. What if someone was in there? Carefully, she began to slide one of the panels open but froze as she heard footsteps approaching on the gravel path.

"Beckie!" Ana called in a hoarse whisper. "Get out of there!"

"What are you doing here?" Rebecca said.

"I didn't want to look for the teahouse alone," Ana said, "so I circled back to get you. If you get us into any more trouble . . ." Her voice trailed off.

Rebecca didn't need to guess what Ana would say next. If she were caught going into the little hut, Ana would be furious. She had to act fast. "Maybe there's nothing important inside," Rebecca said, "or maybe—"

"Maybe there's a soo-koo living there!" Ana said, finishing Rebecca's sentence in a shaky voice.

Her heart thumping, Rebecca carefully slid the door panels open. The hut was dark and quiet inside. She bent forward and peered in.

"Oh, piffle!" she said with disappointment.

"There's nothing in here except an empty bushel basket, and a messy pile of old blankets and work clothes." She slid the doors closed and returned to the gate. "This must be just a fancy storage area." She looked around. "Now, how am I going to get back over the fence?"

"You should have thought of that sooner," Ana said. "If you don't get out of there fast, I'm leaving—and this time I'm going to tell Mr. Tanaka."

Rebecca searched until she found another large rock near the back corner of the fenced area. She stepped up, got her balance, and then jumped over the fence, landing in a heap of dried pine needles. She brushed herself off.

"Now, let's get out of here before someone catches us," Ana urged.

The cousins hurried down to the lower walkway that led around the pond.

Rebecca pointed to an open-sided building jutting out into the water. "That must be the teahouse," she said. "It almost looks as if it's floating."

A Discovery in the Woods

The entrance was framed by branches covered in clusters of pink cherry blossoms. The boughs cascaded toward the water, making Rebecca wonder if Mr. Tanaka had trained them that way. A stone basin filled with water nestled at the base of the tree, sparkling in the dappled sunlight.

As the girls stepped up to the doorway, Rebecca saw Mrs. Tanaka rubbing mud from her silk slippers with a cloth. On her feet, she wore odd white ankle socks that had separate sections for her big toes. Rebecca thought they looked like mittens for her feet. She couldn't help giggling at the thought.

Mrs. Tanaka looked up with shocked surprise. "Path not kind to shoes," she said hastily, placing the delicate slippers outside the doorway to dry. She turned to the girls and asked irritably, "No work to do?"

Rebecca tried to remember the greeting Mrs. Tanaka had used yesterday morning. Speaking a word in Japanese might make her friendlier.

"Ko-nee-chee-wah," Rebecca said, sounding out the word and making a short bow. "Mr. Tanaka wanted us to see how you make the ikebana." She didn't mention anything about the toppled lantern or keeping out of sight of Miss Ward.

Mrs. Tanaka bowed slightly in return. "You sit," she said, gesturing to long benches that lined the inside of the teahouse. "No talk." *Maybe speaking the new word helped,* Rebecca thought. At least Mrs. Tanaka hadn't turned them away.

In every direction, stunning views of the gardens appeared, as if they were paintings hung in the wooden frames of the structure's open sides.

Rebecca turned back to watch Mrs. Tanaka. With curved scissors, she trimmed leaves from some flower stalks and began to place them in a shallow pot. The stems seemed to be standing upright by themselves, and Rebecca couldn't figure out how. She peered over Mrs. Tanaka's sleeve, and when the gardener's wife noticed how inquisitive Rebecca was, she showed the girls the inside of the pot. Hidden under the water was a metal base with prongs sticking up. Each flower stalk was held tightly in its grip, yet the prongs remained hidden, making it seem as if the flowers were growing from the pot. Rebecca smiled. The idea wasn't too different from the posts that remained under water at the island to support the stepping-stones, but Rebecca kept the thought to herself. She didn't want to remind Mrs. Tanaka of what had happened yesterday.

The cousins watched Mrs. Tanaka arrange purple orchids alongside one bare, twisting branch. The design was so simple yet so striking. The girls began to clap, but Mrs. Tanaka didn't even smile.

"Mr. Tanaka very busy?" she asked. The girls nodded. "This is good," she said. "You stay away."

Rebecca sensed Mrs. Tanaka's annoyance. If only she could think of a way to change Mrs. Tanaka's opinion of her. For now, she tried simply to change the subject. Rebecca pointed to the crimson arch she had spied from the fern garden. It loomed even larger from the teahouse and seemed close by. "What is that?" she asked. For the first time, she saw Mrs. Tanaka smile faintly.

"This is *torii*," she said.

"Toe-ree?" Rebecca repeated.

"Tells travelers that *Inari* shrine is close by," said Mrs. Tanaka.

Everything at the Japanese Garden fascinated Rebecca. It seemed that whenever she learned one thing, another question arose. She had no idea what an Inari shrine was.

Seeing her puzzled expression, Mrs. Tanaka tried to explain. "Inari is god of plants. Shrine is where we give thanks to Inari for things that grow."

So that's what the mysterious little building was—a shrine! Rebecca gave Ana a secret nudge, but Ana turned her face away. Mrs. Tanaka walked to the corner of the teahouse and placed the flower arrangement on a tall stand. While her back was turned, Rebecca leaned in and whispered to Ana. "So, the little building is fenced off because it's a shrine, and the two fox statues must be guarding the god of plants."

"They certainly weren't guarding any clues," Ana hissed. "You could have gotten us into big trouble for nothing!"

"There was no way to know that before I checked," Rebecca mumbled.

Their whispered conversation drew Mrs. Tanaka's attention. She pointed abruptly to the entrance. "Now," she commanded, "time to go." As the girls hurried out she warned, "Do not make trouble!"

Rebecca's cheeks felt hot. Mrs. Tanaka had good reason to be unhappy with her, but the more she thought about it, the more it seemed that the gardener's wife had turned against the girls the moment she met them—well before Rebecca had fallen into the pond, and before the fern had tumbled from the lunch box. If Aunt Fannie had thought that having the girls'

company would help soften the Tanakas'
sadness for the son they had lost, she was
mistaken.

At the edge of the path, Rebecca stopped
beside a low bush covered with clusters of
deep purple blossoms. While Ana went ahead,
Rebecca looked back at the teahouse. Perhaps
she should apologize to the gardener's wife for
everything that had happened, even if most of
it really wasn't her fault. But Mrs. Tanaka had
already turned away.

Rebecca was about to walk on when she
noticed some tools tossed under the lower
branches of the bush. A shovel with unfamiliar
symbols carved into its wooden handle was
pushed into a small pile of yellowed leaves. Bits
of wet grass stuck to its blade. Beside it a small
spade lay caked in mud. *A soo-koo wouldn't be
happy about these at all,* Rebecca mused. *But then,
no one here seems happy today.*

A Discovery in the Woods

That evening when the girls returned to the apartment, Rebecca heaved a sigh of relief. Ana sliced some *hallah* bread onto a plate and put it on the table with a pot of honey to spread on top.

"At least you didn't get us into any real trouble today," Ana said quietly, "but you could have! You shouldn't have snooped in the shrine." She stopped talking as Aunt Fannie came into the room.

"How was day at garden?" Aunt Fannie asked. She stroked Rebecca's hair. "Today you are dry, at least," she said with a laugh.

Rebecca forced a smile. She couldn't let Aunt Fannie find out about everything that had gone wrong the day before.

"I think you are maybe tired," Aunt Fannie said, "but some chores I need." She pointed to a bowl of potatoes and a large bunch of carrots. "Please to peel and cut," she said. "This will be big help to me."

"Sure," the girls said, finishing their snack and clearing the table. Ana found two paring knives, and they set to work at the sink. Ana peeled as fast as she could and then suddenly dropped her knife in the sink.

"You can finish," she said. "I'm going down to check my plants."

"Wait for me," Rebecca said.

"I don't need any help," Ana declared and hurried out.

Rebecca continued to peel the vegetables, feeling abandoned. When Aunt Fannie came into the kitchen, Rebecca tried to look as if nothing was wrong. "Ana went to her garden," she said quickly. "I'll catch up in a few minutes."

Aunt Fannie pulled a small brass key from her pocket and handed it to Rebecca. "This I find on edge of tub. Is not ours, so must belong to you."

"I found it at the bottom of the sink," Rebecca said, puzzled. Her mind flashed back to Nathaniel's smock, which had been hanging over the sink. The key must be his, she realized. Rebecca took the key and dropped it into her dress pocket. "I'll find out where it belongs," she told her aunt. *And,* she promised herself, *I'll also find out if this has anything to do with what's been going on at the Japanese Garden.*

"You go to Ana now," Aunt Fannie said. "It is beautiful day. Better to be outside than in."

Rebecca dashed down the stairs and found Ana in the backyard examining a spade and hoe that were propped against the garden fence. The missing tools! Rebecca was surprised and relieved that her cousin had found them.

"Your tools have returned!" she said.

But Ana didn't look as pleased as Rebecca had expected.

"I'm not sure they're mine," Ana said uncertainly. "The handle on the hoe is different, and the spade has shiny new bolts."

"Well, at least you can work in your garden now," Rebecca said, trying to cheer her up.

"It's too late to work out here now. It's almost suppertime." Ana frowned. "And tomorrow we'll be at the Japanese Garden with the Tanakas."

"Well, why don't we water the seedlings?" Rebecca suggested.

"Yes, maybe we should," Ana agreed grudgingly. "It has been warm the past three days, and the plants might be . . . how do you say?" She stuck out her tongue and let her head loll to the side.

"Thirsty?" Rebecca guessed.

"Yes, thirsty," Ana said, "but also . . ." She flopped her head down and let her arms hang loose.

"Oh, I know," Rebecca exclaimed. "The plants might have *wilted*!"

"Yes," Ana said. "*Wilted*. You're good with words." Then she added, "Not so good with following instructions."

Rebecca flinched. She had helped Ana with her English from the first day she had arrived in New York. Her cousin had known very few words then. Now she spoke English with barely any difficulty and learned new words as quickly as a rag soaking up water. Rebecca doubted she could learn to speak another language so fast. She admired Ana and wished she could find a way to bring them closer again.

"How do the seedlings look today?" Rebecca asked.

"The cold frame was already open," Ana said tersely. She bent down and poked her finger into the pots. "They aren't wilted—they're nice and damp. Someone—or something—watered them."

"So, the soo-koo has returned with tools and water," Rebecca said, smiling.

"Phooey," Ana scoffed and headed back to the apartment.

8

THE SPRITE IN THE GARDEN

At dinner, Rebecca poked at her food.
Everything tasted flat, including the knishes she
had made the evening before. She and Ana ate
in silence as the rest of the family chattered.
Afterward, Ana's brothers, Josef and Michael,
walked to the corner store to pick up an evening
newspaper.

"You left a candle burning in the shed out
back," Josef chided the girls when he and
Michael returned.

There's a light inside the shed? Rebecca thought.
Ana seemed to be thinking the same thing. She
set aside her book, and the girls looked at each
other with surprise.

"Let's go check the backyard," Rebecca said
to Ana when the brothers had gone into their

room. "We can look for signs of the soo-koo. If there is such a thing, maybe it left another clue."

"You're always looking for clues," Ana grumped, turning back to the book she was reading. "You can go by yourself if you want to."

"Just think," Rebecca said, "we might actually see a soo-koo! I wonder what it would look like—a person, or a gnome, or a hairy beast? We could be the first people in America to find out."

Outside the window, sunset had turned the sky violet. Rebecca jumped up and headed for the door. "Well, I'm going to spy on the garden, even if you aren't," she declared. "Maybe I'll discover who took your tools—and who's been working out there."

Ana slid off her chair. "We're going to check the garden," she called to her parents. "We'll be right back!"

"Again with the plants?" Aunt Fannie questioned. "Seedlings are not babies to be checked every minute." The cousins stood by the door, waiting for permission. "Go, but don't stay long. Is getting dark."

Outside, the girls stole along the side of the building to the backyard. Then Ana hesitated. "I'm going back. It really is getting dark," she said quietly.

Rebecca didn't want Ana to leave so soon. She hoped that sharing this small adventure might bring them closer. She said, "I think that's when the soo-koo would come out, don't you?"

"I guess so," Ana whispered. "If there is one."

The girls huddled in the shadows, watching for any movement. Instead, they heard a faint clicking noise.

Snick. Snick.

Rebecca stiffened. "Do you hear that?"

"I wonder if there are rats in the compost pile," Ana murmured. "That would be really creepy."

Rebecca moved stealthily toward the mysterious sounds. "I don't think the noise is coming from the compost pile," she whispered. "I think there's something inside the shed. Maybe that's why Josef saw a light."

"I've had enough snooping around in the dark," said Ana. She turned back toward the apartment building.

"Don't leave now," Rebecca said. "Look!" She pointed to the shed door. The padlock dangled from its latch.

"It's unlocked!" Ana breathed.

"Follow me," Rebecca whispered. They crept around the back of the shed toward a pale beam of light that reflected against the wall of the building next door. It glimmered against the bricks like a ghost.

Together, Ana and Rebecca inched their way along the narrow space between the fence and the building and peered at the back of the shed.

"Windows!" Ana said softly.

Although the front of the shed facing the garden was a solid wall, two large windows faced the back. The flickering light they had

seen was coming from inside—and so was the
eerie sound. *Snick. Snick.* Rebecca shuddered.
It sounded like biting teeth. Her heart thumped
wildly. What if they encountered something that
wasn't human?

In the deepening shadows, she stumbled on
a metal washtub. She dragged it close to the
window, turned it upside down, and climbed
up. Ana stepped up beside her onto the over-
turned tub. Balancing gingerly, the girls pressed
close to the window glass and peered in.

A dark figure stood silhouetted in the
gloomy light. A kerosene lantern sat on a table
in front of a series of twisted shapes that cast
long, crooked shadows on the wall behind them.

The dark figure raised an arm, and the
lamplight glinted off curved metal where a
hand should be. "It has claws!" Rebecca cried
in alarm. "Run!"

She jumped from her perch, but just as Ana
turned away from the window, the tub tipped
over with an ear-splitting clatter. She tumbled
to the ground, and Rebecca knelt to help her.

THE SPRITE IN THE GARDEN

The shed door banged open, and a figure rushed out and loomed over the girls. Trembling and hugging her cousin, Rebecca forced herself to look up. Standing over her was not a ghostly sprite, as she had feared—but Mr. Tanaka.

"Why are you out here in the dark?" he demanded.

Rebecca stared up at him, dumbfounded. "What are *you* doing here?" she sputtered. "You scared us half to death!" Rebecca helped her cousin up and brushed bits of grass from her dress.

"I will show you," Mr. Tanaka said in a soft voice. He pushed up his glasses. The dim light hid his eyes behind the thick lenses. Still, Rebecca could feel him staring at her. "But you must promise not to tell anyone what you see inside."

"How can we promise when we don't know what you're doing?" Rebecca asked.

"So many questions," said Mr. Tanaka, leading the girls around the shed to the open door. Inside, a lantern cast a dim yellow light.

A GROWING SUSPICION

Rebecca cautiously stepped in and saw what had made the strange, crooked shadows: rows of tiny potted trees lined up on a shelf against the wall. Rebecca had never seen such perfect miniature trees before. They looked small enough to fit in the palm of her hand. "You're growing little trees?" she asked.

"These are *bonsai*," Mr. Tanaka said, facing the narrow shelves. The girls exchanged glances, perplexed. "It is another Japanese art using plants," he said.

Mr. Tanaka took down one of the trees. It was planted in a hollowed branch, and thin copper wires supported its twiggy limbs. The tree arched as if an ocean wind had swept the branches to one side.

"This reminds me of the trees that you trained to grow in a certain direction at the Japanese Garden," Rebecca said.

"Exactly right," Mr. Tanaka said, nodding his head. "In America, only a few have seen them. Bonsai are trees that are shaped to stay small. Wires guide them in a certain direction, and they must be pruned just so." He held up a pair of sharp pruning shears and made a clipping motion in the air.

"Those clippers sounded like teeth," Rebecca blurted out. "And when the lamplight reflected off the blades, I thought they were claws!"

The gardener spread his arms in apology. "I never meant to scare you. How could I know you were outside the window?" He picked up a few tiny twigs. "See," he said, "I was clipping extra branches."

"I still don't understand why you're out here," Rebecca bristled. Had Mr. Tanaka stolen these trees from the plant house? Where else could they have come from?

"I will explain," said the gardener. "I have been cultivating these bonsai for my own pleasure for quite some time. Before long, I had too many in our apartment. Where to put them? Then I looked inside this shed." He waved his arm in the direction of the shelves. "The windows let in the afternoon light, and there were many shelves."

"Did you put on the padlock?" Ana asked.

Mr. Tanaka looked down at the floor, as if he was ashamed. "I could not let the landlord find out. Do you think he would allow a tenant to start a business here without paying rent?" he asked.

"I thought you said the bonsais were a hobby," Rebecca countered. "That's not a business."

"Now they must become my work," Mr. Tanaka said. He was silent for a moment and then confided, "I think I will lose my job very soon."

"Lose your job?" Ana echoed. "But why? The Japanese Garden needs you."

"The Japanese Garden has been open for a year now, and fewer workers are needed. In the beginning, different parts of the garden had to be built—fences and carved gates, bridges, waterfalls. Now it is done, and already many workers have been let go. You heard Mr. Gager. I believe that soon my skills will no longer be needed and I will be next."

THE SPRITE IN THE GARDEN

The gardener sat down heavily on a wooden stool. "I worked diligently on the proper design of the Japanese Garden," he said. "I made certain everything was done in the traditional way." His mouth turned up in a rueful smile. "So everything is going along too well. Mr. Gager thinks it all happens without any effort."

"Can't you explain that, so he will understand?" Ana asked.

"I have tried many things to ensure that my skills will be needed," Mr. Tanaka answered. "I created the small sand garden as a model so that the director would want me to build a larger one. I took no time from my regular duties, but came early and stayed late. I expected no extra pay, but I had much hope. But Mr. Gager is taking a long time to consider whether visitors would like such a garden and whether there is money to pay for it."

Now Rebecca thought she understood why Mrs. Tanaka didn't want them to bother Mr. Tanaka or cause him any problems. She was trying to protect his job, too.

"I didn't mean to cause so much trouble," Rebecca said earnestly.

"Most of the problems were not your fault," replied Mr. Tanaka. "As you know, there was already damage before you visited. No one can figure out who is doing these things. It is as if an angry tsukumogami is damaging the gardens instead of helping."

"I still don't understand where the bonsais fit in," Ana said.

"It is simple," the gardener said. "Mrs. Tanaka and I are worried about what to do if I lose my job, so we had the idea of turning the bonsai into a small business. I hope to persuade Mr. Gager to set up a display of this rare art. It would draw many admirers! If he agrees, perhaps I can sell my bonsai to the Botanic Garden. Maybe I can sell some to collectors, too, and earn enough to live."

"I think I'm beginning to understand," Rebecca said. "If you sold the bonsai plants, then you'd be using the shed to run a business."

"Exactly," said Mr. Tanaka. "If the landlord

discovers this, I will have no place to work.
I don't have enough money saved to pay extra
rent for the shed." He looked up. "I tried to keep
you from working in your garden so that you
wouldn't discover my secret—at least until
I could convince Mr. Gager to display the bonsai. I was afraid you might tell someone."

"Did you take my tools?" Ana asked.

Mr. Tanaka nodded. "I only meant to borrow
them, but the handle on the hoe cracked, and
the spade handle was quite loose. To make up
for using them, I fixed them both."

"But why did you need the tools?" Rebecca
asked. "Were you the one who weeded in Ana's
garden?"

Mr. Tanaka nodded again. "I thought
I would prepare your garden bed so that you
would have no reason to spend time there."

"You said it was a sprite," Ana said. "We
came down tonight to try to see it."

"I ask for forgiveness. I did not mean to scare
you with old tales." Mr. Tanaka had a faraway
look in his eyes. "When I was a boy, my father

told me of the tsukumogami. I made sure to take good care of all tools. I always wished to find favor with the sprite one day." He looked up. "In Japan, many believe in these helpful sprites."

"So *you're* our soo-koo," Rebecca said. "You did all our work without being seen." For a moment, Rebecca couldn't help wondering what else Mr. Tanaka might have done. Could he be responsible for the damage in the Japanese Garden? Could he have placed the fern in Ana's lunch box? No, she decided. The gardener would never cause problems in the garden he loved. It was also impossible to believe that Mr. Tanaka, who had been so kind, would do anything to hurt them.

"If we can still be friends," said Mr. Tanaka, "we will have a busy day at the Japanese Garden tomorrow. There is so much work to be done. I must finish repairing the bamboo fence and fix the stepping-stone in the pond. Then there are the ferns that must be replanted near the stone lantern. And you two must finish planting the fern garden."

Rebecca's heart sank. Just the mention of the broken fence and stepping-stone made her miserable. It reminded her of the mistakes she had made—and of the fact that her friendship with Ana needed mending, too.

If only she could prove their innocence once and for all. Then she might finally win back Ana's trust.

Suddenly, Rebecca knew exactly what she had to do.

9
A KEY AND A CLUE

"We have to go to the gardens before the Tanakas tomorrow morning," Rebecca said once they reached the apartment.

"Why?" Ana asked, her voice doubtful.

"We need to scout around without Mr. Tanaka or Miss Ward watching us," Rebecca said. "It's the only way we'll have a chance to figure out who has been damaging things. If we can figure out who's sabotaging the garden, then we'll know who sabotaged us!"

Ana bristled. "Your plans keep getting us into trouble. This is just another scheme that could backfire. I'm not snooping around the Japanese Garden again. If we got caught there when it's closed, I don't know what would happen."

"How could the punishment be any worse?" Rebecca reasoned. "If we can't clear our names, we might as well just stay home."

"Maybe *you* should stay," Ana retorted. "If I go to the Japanese Garden by myself, at least I can show how reliable I am. I won't have you to mess things up."

"You can't mean that!" Rebecca cried. She slumped onto Ana's bed. "You have to forgive me for going onto the island," she pleaded. "That was really the only mistake I made. Falling into the pond was an accident!"

Ana turned her back.

"You don't think I put the fern in the lunch box, do you?" Rebecca asked. She was almost afraid to hear her cousin's answer.

Ana faced Rebecca with a guilty look. "Oh, Beckie, I—I'm sorry. I truly don't blame you for that, but everything has just gone so wrong!"

"We still have a chance to make things right," Rebecca insisted, getting up. "If we find the real culprit, no one will doubt us again. I'm sure Miss Ward would even let you take classes this summer. I know it's risky, but we've got to try." She put her arm around Ana. "Are you with me?"

Ana didn't pull away, but she still hesitated. "We'd have to get permission to leave here so early," she argued, "and walk all the way there."

"We know the way," Rebecca assured her. "It's not that far, really."

"I just don't know," Ana said, shaking her head. "What about the Tanakas? They would be waiting for us to take the trolley."

"I'll write a note," Rebecca said, "telling them we'll meet them later in the morning. Please, Ana, we've got to stick together." She waited expectantly for her cousin's decision, but Ana didn't say another word.

When Aunt Fannie came to tuck them into bed, Rebecca was surprised to hear Ana ask, "Is it all right if we leave really early tomorrow, Mama? There's something special happening at the Botanic Garden at sunrise."

"What is so special?" Aunt Fannie asked. "Sun comes up every morning."

"There's a lot going on there," Ana said honestly. "We don't want to miss anything."

"I will make your lunch tonight, then," Aunt Fannie said. "And wear a shawl. Mornings are still cold." She placed Nathaniel's freshly pressed smock on a chair along with his laundered socks. "You return these to friend," she told Rebecca.

"Thank you for washing them," Rebecca said. She kissed Aunt Fannie on the cheek.

"Is nothing," Aunt Fannie said. "What is one more shirt in pile of dirty laundry?"

As soon as Aunt Fannie closed the bedroom door, Rebecca said, "You won't be sorry. We're going to get to the bottom of things tomorrow." Ana's silence in the darkness told Rebecca that her cousin was still uncertain about the plan.

Rebecca awoke the next morning before the sun came up. She nudged Ana, who jumped out of bed. The girls tried not to make a sound, but as Rebecca pulled on her dress she heard a metallic *clink*, as if a metal button had fallen to the floor. The key! She knelt down, feeling around until her fingers closed on it.

She had a hunch that the key was important, but she didn't quite know why. She slipped it back into her pocket, stuffed Nathaniel's clothes into an oilcloth bag, and tiptoed into the kitchen.

The cousins took their lunch box and two breakfast rolls from the pantry. Rebecca slipped her note under the Tanakas' door, and the girls stole down the staircase, out into the chilly morning air.

Rebecca slung the bag with Nathaniel's clothes over her shoulder and nibbled her roll as they hurried along Flatbush Avenue. A milk wagon passed, pulled by a thin horse. The deliveryman seemed half-asleep as the horse stopped out of habit at each building along the route. Soon the girls had left the wagon behind. The road seemed almost deserted.

Just when Rebecca was beginning to think it really was too far to walk, she spied the black gates that led into the Botanic Garden. She and Ana slipped through a break in the hedges and made their way along the path.

"It's too easy to get in here," Ana remarked. "Anyone could have come in and caused damage without being noticed."

"That's true," Rebecca agreed, "but the troublemaker seems to know the Japanese Garden well. I wonder if it's someone who used to work there."

They passed the darkened building beside the Children's Garden, the glass plant house, and the wide lawns with trees silhouetted against the sky, which was only beginning to grow light.

"Everything looks so different now," Ana said. "I hope we don't get lost."

Birds chattered and flitted between the trees. A damp breeze rustled the leaves, and it seemed as if it might rain. Rebecca felt a shiver race along the back of her neck, but she tried to act confident. She didn't want to spook her cousin. Rebecca moved closer and linked her arm through Ana's. She was heartened when her cousin didn't pull away.

A Growing Suspicion

The girls stopped at the fork in the path. "Where should we go first?" Ana asked.

"I'm not sure . . ." Rebecca said. She shoved her hand into her pocket and withdrew the brass key. "I'm pretty sure this fell from Nathaniel's smock," she said, showing the key to Ana. "I think it might be a clue."

Rebecca held the key up to the growing light. Ana studied it for a moment and then her eyes widened. "What about the shrine? There was a lock on the gate. And that's near the spot where we heard Nathaniel arguing with someone, remember?"

"You're right," Rebecca said, pocketing the key. "Let's go." The girls headed to the left and began climbing the sloping path to the shrine.

Gray light filtered through the treetops, forming misty beams that slanted to the ground. The clouds overhead were thick but seemed outlined with a faint glow. Rebecca was glad the sky was growing lighter, but she kept to the edge of the path, deep in the shadows. If anyone was around, she didn't want to be seen.

A barking sound drew her along until the wooden shrine appeared, looking even more mysterious in the dim light than it had the previous day. Ana clutched Rebecca's hand. "Do you think one of the fox statues might have a sprite inside?" she asked, and Rebecca gave a nervous giggle at the thought. The girls crouched behind a thick stand of pine trees and peered out. The foxes kept their stony gaze, and the barking echoed inside the shrine. Then Rebecca heard the scraping sound of wood sliding against wood. The doors to the tiny building were opening! *No animal could do that,* Rebecca thought.

While the girls watched, as still and quiet as the stone foxes, a wiry form emerged from inside the shrine, jumped down the steps, and leaped over the picket fence, landing with a heavy *thud*. Suddenly, the figure bent over in a fit of coughing. It was Nathaniel!

After he had disappeared down the hill toward the main area of the Botanic Garden, Rebecca approached the gate. It was locked, as she had expected. Rebecca pushed the key into the rusty padlock and gave it a firm twist, and the lock fell open with a click.

Rebecca pushed open the creaking gate. Ana huddled close as Rebecca slid the shrine doors open and crawled inside. There was barely enough space to stretch out. A basket held folded blankets, and a pile of clothes was stacked in the corner. No wonder Nathaniel had been able to find an extra pair of socks, thought Rebecca.

She backed out and closed the door. "It's not being used for storage, as I thought yesterday," she said. "I think Nathaniel has been sleeping in here!" Ana's eyes widened.

"He never did say where he lives," Rebecca continued, "and he's always here so early. I don't know where he got this key, but he must have been using it to get inside."

"No matter how nice he seems," Ana declared, "he could be the one who got us into trouble by walking on the sand garden after we raked it. And he sure could have hidden the fern pot in our lunch box."

Maybe Nathaniel is trying to get rid of us,
Rebecca thought. It seemed almost everyone
wanted them out of the way. Mr. Tanaka had
wanted them out of Ana's backyard garden,
Miss Ward wanted them to leave the Botanic
Garden because she thought they were creating
mischief, and even Mrs. Tanaka didn't seem to
want them there. But why would Nathaniel
want them sent home?

Rebecca looked at the bag holding Nathaniel's
smock, as if it held an answer, but all she could
think of were more questions. What was
Nathaniel doing in the shrine? What had he
been arguing about yesterday, and with whom?
And if he *had* trampled the sand garden, how
could he have made the small, shallow footprints they'd seen there? It still seemed far more
likely that those footprints belonged to the
well-dressed woman, the one who had also
taken the orchid.

"We can't rule out the woman in the fancy
hat just yet," Rebecca reminded Ana. "She and
the man she was with had no business being

in the sand garden, or taking flowers."

"That's true," said Ana. "Still, maybe we should follow Nathaniel and see what he's up to."

Rebecca closed the gate and locked it behind them. The girls hurried along the path they had seen the young man take. It led them into a part of the garden they had never before explored.

In just a few moments, they spotted him but kept a good distance behind.

Without warning, a sharp *knock* split the air, startling Rebecca. She and Ana exchanged worried looks. "What's that?" Ana whispered in a trembling voice.

Before she could guess, Rebecca heard the strange sound again. *Knock!*

It was far too early for any workers to be in the area. Except for Nathaniel, Rebecca thought she and Ana were alone. She pushed thoughts of tool sprites and other spirits from her mind. They couldn't be real. Hadn't Mr. Tanaka more or less admitted that?

"I don't know what that could be," she finally

answered, "but what if it means more trouble?" Drizzle misted the air, and she pulled her shawl tighter.

Ana glanced up at the sky, which was thick with dark clouds. "We can't stay out much longer," she said. "Maybe we should split up. I'll follow Nathaniel, and you find out what that sound is."

Rebecca gulped. She didn't want to go into the woods on her own, but weren't they here to discover who was behind the damage? She turned from the path into an area where the trees were thicker, and the light barely penetrated. A gloomy rock formation loomed up. Rebecca hunkered behind it to listen for the mysterious sounds. The noise was louder now. *Knock!* Rebecca must be getting closer.

Suddenly, a lavender-clad figure stepped from a stand of trees. It was Mrs. Tanaka! What was she doing in this isolated place so early? *She's not making a flower arrangement now,* Rebecca thought.

Mrs. Tanaka looked around furtively, as if

checking to see if anyone was nearby, and then moved on, her kimono swishing as it brushed the ground.

Rebecca slunk from her hiding place. She tried to keep pace with Mrs. Tanaka as she wound her way between the trees, but quickly lost sight of her. *Which way next?* Rebecca wondered. If she became lost in the woods, how would she find her way out? Rebecca had barely paid attention to the way she had come. She had to find Mrs. Tanaka again, if only to follow her back to a familiar path.

Rebecca wished that she and Ana had stayed together. Now that she was alone, the strange sounds were more alarming. The rhythmic clacking grew louder as she pushed ahead.

Soon the knocking noise was joined by the sound of water splashing. Rebecca peeked through the knobby stalks of a clump of bamboo, half wondering if she might actually discover a garden sprite at work. Instead, she saw Mrs. Tanaka standing beside a small stream. In the water was a curious contraption—a large, hollow pipe of dried bamboo suspended on a frame made of smaller lengths of bamboo. The pipe was like a scoop that caught water as it flowed over a small stone ledge. When water filled the pipe, it grew heavy and tipped down, spilling the water gently into a rippling pool, then tipping back up and knocking against the stone ledge. The device was like a moving fountain!

As she blinked into the mist, Rebecca saw Mrs. Tanaka lean over the clacking fountain. From her wide sleeve, she pulled a short spade that looked like the tool Rebecca had spotted under the shrub near the teahouse. Mrs. Tanaka grasped the bamboo pipe firmly with one hand and pushed the point of the spade between the twists of raffia twine that held it to the frame. She pulled and pried, but the binding held fast.

For a moment, the gardener's wife seemed uncertain what to do next. Then she pulled harder and flinched as the entire frame suddenly crumpled. The pipe flew from her hands and fell with a loud crack on the rocks below.

A Growing Suspicion

Without the pipe to slow its flow, water rushed in a torrent from the stream above, tumbling noisily into the pool.

How could the gardener's wife do such a thing? Horrified, Rebecca wondered what to do. Should she confront Mrs. Tanaka right then, or should she wait until Miss Ward arrived and tell her what she had seen? She knew it would be her word against Mrs. Tanaka's, and she knew who Miss Ward was most likely to believe. The stern teacher already suspected Rebecca of creating mischief, and when Rebecca had tried to report the woman who'd taken the orchid, no one had seemed interested at all.

Mrs. Tanaka hurried away, her silk slippers barely visible beneath her kimono. Rebecca trailed cautiously behind. Careful to stay out of sight, she tried to follow Mrs. Tanaka's faint footprints in the soft, damp earth.

Scanning the ground ahead of her for the prints reminded Rebecca of her first day at the Botanic Garden, when she had made her ill-considered visit to the island to search for footprints.

She hadn't found any there, but the memory jogged a flash of recognition: *these* footprints were small and light—just like the prints in the sand garden.

Had *Mrs. Tanaka* been the one who had walked on the carefully raked sand pattern? Such a possibility would never have occurred to Rebecca, but now that she had seen the gardener's wife break the fountain, she began to wonder. All the damage had taken place in the Japanese Garden, where Mrs. Tanaka spent her day. At the teahouse, Rebecca had seen Mrs. Tanaka cleaning mud from her silk shoes— mud that could have come from the soil around the lantern and fern garden. Even someone as slight as Mrs. Tanaka could have toppled the stone lantern if she had pushed hard enough. And the gardener's wife had been alone in the side room with the girls' lunch box before the fern fell out. With each footprint, Rebecca felt more certain that Mrs. Tanaka could have been the culprit. The only thing she had no answer for was why.

A GROWING SUSPICION

Rebecca stayed out of sight as the gardener's wife reached the bridge next to the waterfall. Instead of crossing, Mrs. Tanaka paused to gaze over the railing into the water below. Then, with a muffled cry, she turned away and rushed toward the teahouse.

Baffled and a little frightened, Rebecca ran to find Ana and tell her what she had seen. She had just rounded the first bend in the path when Ana came rushing toward her, out of breath.

"I followed Nathaniel to the Children's Garden," Ana blurted out. "Through the window, I saw him take some biscuits from the cupboard and drink some milk from the icebox. I had to duck when he turned around, and the next time I peeked inside, he was gone. I looked everywhere and couldn't find him at all."

Rebecca steadied her hands on her cousin's shoulders. "Ana," she said solemnly, "I saw something far worse. There's been more damage, and I saw who did it."

"What happened?" Ana asked.

"I hardly know where to begin," Rebecca

said. She took a deep breath. "That knocking sound turned out to be a kind of bamboo fountain. While I was secretly watching it, Mrs. Tanaka appeared from nowhere and used a spade to cut the twine that held it together. The pieces fell apart, and the pipe cracked on some rocks. She broke the fountain!"

Ana gasped. "We have to tell Miss Ward as soon as she arrives."

As they hurried toward the plant house to await Miss Ward, Rebecca tried to push away her fear of not being believed. She knew that her only choice was to describe what she had seen and trust that Miss Ward would realize it was the truth. Just as she managed to convince herself of this, a more disturbing thought came to mind. She stopped abruptly.

"Oh, Ana, I've been so worried that the others won't believe me. But what if they *do*? They might blame Mr. Tanaka for the fact that we sneaked in this morning. They might even hold him responsible for what his wife did. He could lose his job on the spot!"

A Growing Suspicion

A sinking feeling roiled Rebecca's stomach. It had been so unfair to be falsely accused, and so awful to have Ana angry with her as a result. All she had wanted to do was solve the mystery. Now that she had, she really didn't feel any better.

Before she could begin to think of a solution to their dilemma, a shrill whistle cut the silence around them. Rebecca was surprised to see Nathaniel racing along the path that Rebecca had followed earlier. Then Miss Ward and Mr. Gager strode up behind the girls. Rebecca felt as if they were suddenly surrounded.

"Follow me," Nathaniel ordered. He led the group to the stream where the fountain lay in pieces. He pointed accusingly at the girls. "You're not going to get away with this!"

Rebecca felt rooted to the ground as Nathaniel fished the bamboo pieces from the water and handed them to Mr. Gager.

"You've got it all wrong," she protested, before words failed her.

10
BANISHED!

"I'm taking you girls home this moment," Miss Ward announced. "Your family will be held responsible for the damage you've caused. This is the last time you will set foot in this garden."

"If Nathaniel had seen what really happened here, he wouldn't try to pin it on us," Rebecca insisted. "I'm sorry to tell you this—really, I am—but I saw who broke the fountain. It was—"

Mr. Gager cut her off. "It's time you take responsibility for all you've done," he declared. "You've broken the rules simply by being here unsupervised." He turned to Miss Ward. "I'll tend to your classes this morning while you escort these troublemakers home."

A GROWING SUSPICION

Miss Ward ushered the girls away. Ana began to cry quietly, and Rebecca tried to hold back the tears that were filling her own eyes. In a last desperate attempt to tell what she had seen, Rebecca turned back to the director.

"You just have to listen to me," she pleaded. "You're not being fair!"

Mr. Gager folded his arms across his chest. "I've heard enough," he said firmly. He looked at the darkening sky and addressed Miss Ward. "You'd better accompany them home immediately, before the rain hits."

That was my last chance, Rebecca thought dismally. *Even discovering the real culprit wasn't enough.*

As Miss Ward grasped Rebecca's hand to urge her along, the oilcloth bag over her shoulder slipped to her wrist. She still had Nathaniel's clothes! Rebecca pulled her hand free, tugged Nathaniel's things from the bag, and offered them to him.

"I almost forgot," she said, choking out the words. Then she reached into her pocket and held out the small key. "I'm not sure who should have this," she murmured. "It's for the lock on the gate to the shrine."

Nathaniel's face turned pale.

Mr. Gager snatched the key from her open palm. "Where did you get this, young lady?"

"It fell out of Nathaniel's pocket when my aunt washed his smock," she said. Ana moved beside her and took her hand.

Mr. Gager's angry gaze turned from Rebecca to Nathaniel. "How did you get this, young man? Have you been involved in the problems we've had?"

Miss Ward spoke before Nathaniel could answer. "I recently discovered that Nathaniel has been sleeping in the shrine overnight."

"Sleeping there?" repeated Mr. Gager. He sounded incredulous.

"I confronted him yesterday," Miss Ward went on. "When he explained that he had nowhere to live, I held off on reporting him while I tried to find a better solution." She stuffed her hands into the pockets of her sweater. "I gave him permission to take some milk and biscuits from the children's area before anyone arrived in the mornings."

So, thought Rebecca, *that was the argument Ana and I overheard near the shrine.* Nathaniel must have been begging Miss Ward not to report him. But why didn't he have anywhere else to live?

A peal of thunder rumbled through the air like the growl of an angry lion, and a smattering of raindrops began to fall. Mr. Gager glanced up at the ominous clouds and gave a weary sigh. "It seems there's more to this story than I realized," he said. He looked at Ana and Rebecca. "Perhaps I have blamed you too quickly. I'm going to need a little more time to sort this all out."

Rebecca felt a surge of hope. Maybe now Mr. Gager would listen to her.

It began to rain steadily. "Quickly," said Miss Ward. "Let's get to the teahouse before we're soaked."

Nathaniel looked ready to run off, but

Mr. Gager fixed him with a piercing gaze. "You're not going anywhere until we get to the bottom of all this."

They rushed along the path around the pond and dashed under the sheltering roof of the teahouse just as the clouds unleashed a downpour. Rebecca saw that Mr. Tanaka had already taken cover there. Then she saw Mrs. Tanaka standing demurely behind a half-finished flower arrangement. Her mouth went dry. Standing in the teahouse reminded Rebecca of how much she'd admired Mrs. Tanaka's graceful manner and her talents. She almost wished she hadn't discovered what the gardener's wife had done. Still, if she didn't tell Mr. Gager and Miss Ward what she had seen, they would continue to blame her and Ana—or turn their suspicions to Nathaniel.

The director shook raindrops from his hat and then faced Nathaniel with a scowl. "You'd better explain yourself, young man."

Nathaniel spoke in a near whisper. "Until recently I lived in an orphanage. I'd been there since I was eight, and it was home to me." His shoulders sagged. "As I got older, I helped out in every way I could. I even started a kitchen garden to raise vegetables, and I realized I loved growing things."

Nathaniel's voice gained a note of pride. "When I learned of the classes here, I asked for permission to come after school and on weekends. This garden became my second home. Then, a few weeks ago, when I turned sixteen, the orphanage turned me out. I was too old to stay any longer." Nathaniel's face clouded over. "Rules are rules, the matron said. She claimed she was sorry, but she walked me to my cot while I gathered my clothes and then escorted me out the door."

Although Rebecca had been angry at Nathaniel for accusing her and Ana, she felt a pang of sorrow for what had happened. She could see that everyone in the room felt sympathy for him, too.

"I had no place to go other than here," Nathaniel continued. "One day I noticed the

key to the shrine hanging in the plant house.
I knew it was wrong, but I took it and moved
inside. It was cold and awfully cramped, but
I thought I could manage until I found a better
place to live."

Mr. Gager looked pointedly at Nathaniel.
"But why on earth would you damage the
gardens?"

"I didn't!" Nathaniel protested. He looked
crestfallen at Mr. Gager's accusation. "I thought
that if I could find out who was causing all the
damage, I might be rewarded with a job. I've
been stalking the grounds like Sherlock Holmes!
When I saw the broken fountain and found
Rebecca and Ana nearby, I was sure I had found
the culprits." Nathaniel eyed the girls narrowly.
"Maybe I have!"

"You're wrong," Rebecca said, summoning
all her courage.

But before she could explain, Mrs. Tanaka
stepped forward. "Honorable director," she
began, giving a low bow. "Better to speak to
you alone, but must say something and cannot

wait. I cannot allow others to take blame for my wrongs."

Her chin quivered slightly. "It is said that our reflection shows us who we really are. This morning I stopped on bridge and looked into water. I saw anger—and fear. I was ashamed. This is not my nature! I made up my mind to confess terrible things I have done."

Mr. Gager sat heavily on one of the benches and spread his hands in exasperation. "I'm sorry," he said. "I don't understand."

"I am person who caused all problems in Japanese Garden," Mrs. Tanaka said.

"What are you saying, Misako?" Mr. Tanaka asked. "That's impossible!" But one look at the anguish on his wife's face silenced him.

"I have made terrible mistake," she continued, "only trying to save husband's job. I thought with many things to repair, Mr. Tanaka stay very busy. If you need him, you not send him away. Can you not see how important he is? So many skills!"

Mr. Gager shook his head in disbelief, and

Miss Ward seemed stunned. In spite of herself, Rebecca felt sorry for the gardener's wife, especially now that she and Ana had been proven innocent. Mrs. Tanaka must have been desperate to save her husband's job.

"Not want to hurt anyone," Mrs. Tanaka insisted. She turned to Rebecca. "When you fell in pond, I was most sorry! I loosened stone so someone will report the danger—not fall in! Like lantern in fern garden—no one hurt, lantern not broken. Everything can be fixed!" She slumped against Mr. Tanaka's shoulder, and her voice was muffled. "Fountain was last thing. I only meant to cut string. After pipe crash on rocks and fountain fall apart, I knew I must confess. I understand if you will not allow me to return—but please let husband stay! He knew nothing of this."

Rebecca tried to piece everything together, but one thing didn't make sense. "Did you put the fern into our lunch box? How would that help Mr. Tanaka?"

"I did not wish you to get in way of husband's

work," Mrs. Tanaka said. "I also worry you will see how I am causing other damage. Better if Miss Ward sends you home for good." Her voice trailed off.

Mr. Tanaka put his arm around his wife, and she began to sob. "You wanted to help," he said quietly, "but you chose the wrong path."

"I beg you to forgive this foolish woman," Mrs. Tanaka pleaded.

Mr. Gager shook his head in disappointment. "I don't think—" Before the director could finish, Mr. Tanaka broke in.

"Every day," he said, "my only thought is to create beauty for our visitors. I know my wife has always hoped her ikebana arrangements give joy to those who view them. Her mistake was a terrible one, but it was made out of love for me and faith in my work. If you allow me to repair the damage, I can promise such things will never happen again."

The director looked at Mr. Tanaka thoughtfully. "With all the workers who have been let go," he said, "I can see why you were concerned about your job. The truth is, we have come to depend on your skills. We couldn't manage the garden without you. You must repair everything, of course, but your job is secure."

Mr. Tanaka gave a deep sigh. "Out of gratitude," he said, "I have one additional offer. I have been raising bonsai at home and will gladly donate them to the Japanese Garden. If you do not wish to exhibit them, you may sell them to pay for the damage."

"Bonsai?" Mr. Gager stroked his chin thoughtfully. "How intriguing. I had planned to add more features to the Japanese Garden. I haven't forgotten about your sand garden, either. It would blend perfectly with a bonsai display. Why, we'd be the only place on the East Coast to have them."

"Have you decided to add a large sand garden then?" Mr. Tanaka asked, incredulous.

Miss Ward nodded to the director. "Perhaps you should explain how the sand garden has become possible," she suggested.

"I believe I should," he agreed. "We are

about to receive a large donation from a generous banker and his wife. The Van den Meters traveled to Japan not long ago and then came to see our Japanese Garden. I gave them a full tour and permission to wander about wherever they wished. They have fallen in love with it here, especially the demonstration sand garden. In fact, they have offered funding to create a large one for public viewing."

"So that was the mysterious couple we saw in the sand garden," Rebecca said. "But . . . I'm quite sure I saw Mrs. Van den Meter hiding an orchid from the plant house under her coat!"

Mr. Gager and Miss Ward chuckled. "That's entirely possible," said the director. "Our generous benefactor has a prized orchid collection. She often lets us borrow some of her orchids when they are in bloom. We display them until she wants them back. You must have seen her taking one of her own plants home. Since orchids are sensitive to cold temperatures, she was keeping it under wraps to protect it."

Rebecca was relieved that the couple had

been there to help, not steal! More important, their donation had probably secured Mr. Tanaka's job.

Ana spoke up. "What's going to happen to Nathaniel? Can't anyone find a way to help him?"

All eyes turned to the young man.

"You're sixteen, so we might be able to take you on as an apprentice gardener," Mr. Gager began. "But you cannot live here."

Nathaniel's shoulders slumped. Rebecca couldn't imagine where he would go. Surely an apprentice's pay wouldn't cover the rent for even the smallest tenement apartment.

Mr. Tanaka pushed his glasses up on his nose. "Nathaniel cannot sleep in the shrine. Inari is the sacred guardian of plants, but he doesn't run a hotel for gardeners!" He smiled slightly at his own joke and then looked questioningly at his wife. "Now that my job is safe, perhaps Nathaniel could move into the other room in our apartment. Our family is small, but our hearts are large."

A Growing Suspicion

Mrs. Tanaka seemed to brighten for the first time. Rebecca even thought she saw her give Nathaniel a quick, shy smile.

"Do you mean it?" Nathaniel asked.

"You will have to eat my Japanese cooking," Mrs. Tanaka said softly. "You will eat sushi?"

"Real cooking!" Nathaniel exclaimed. "Of course. No more living on biscuits and milk!"

The rain outside slowed to a sprinkle. Mr. Gager pulled out his pocket watch and flipped open its gold cover. "Look at the time! There is so much to be done, and here we are standing about like idlers. The Van den Meters are returning in just two days, and everything must be in perfect order."

Mrs. Tanaka spoke up hesitantly. "When Van den Meters return, please allow me to prepare special tea ceremony. This may be one small way to make up for damage I have caused."

Mr. Gager considered her offer. "That might be permissible," he said.

"Oh, I do think they would enjoy a Japanese

tea ceremony," Miss Ward said. "If it's success-
ful, it might become a public event that we could
have every spring, when the Japanese Garden
is in full bloom."

Rebecca felt encouraged that the director had
not turned down Mrs. Tanaka's offer outright.
Perhaps one day she might regain her place in
the garden as well.

"In the Jewish religion, we have an idea
called *rachmones*," Rebecca said, thinking out
loud. "It's a way to encourage forgiveness.
Maybe we all need a bit of rachmones right
now."

"I will begin by asking for yours," Miss
Ward said to Rebecca and Ana. "I'm terribly
sorry for accusing you." She smiled at Ana.
"To help apologize, I'd be pleased to have you in
my class this summer." She turned to Rebecca.
"And you are welcome to visit any time you are
in Brooklyn."

Ana's face lit up. Rebecca hadn't seen her
cousin so happy in days.

"There is a similar Japanese custom that can

help us move past all that has happened," Mr. Tanaka said. "Come."

The sky had cleared, and the only raindrops now were those sliding off the roof of the teahouse. Mr. Tanaka stepped down to the overflowing stone water basin nestled near the doorway. He bent down and wiped his forehead with a handful of water. "This is a traditional act of forgiveness," he said. "It cleans away mistakes of the past."

Mrs. Tanaka solemnly followed, and Rebecca dipped her own hand into the cool, pure water. As she drew her wet hand across her forehead, she felt a sense of relief wash over her. Ana would be able to attend Miss Ward's classes, and Rebecca would be able to visit whenever she could. Nathaniel could finish his schooling and might eventually have a job at the Botanic Garden. Best of all, he would have a place to live. Mr. Tanaka would have the chance to share his sand garden and his bonsai, and Mrs. Tanaka would earn forgiveness.

After Ana bent over the basin, she hugged

Rebecca tightly and Rebecca hugged her back. "I guess even twins have spats," Ana said, "but they always make up."

"Now, everyone back to work!" Mr. Gager commanded.

As the group headed down the path to the plant house, Rebecca walked alongside Ana. "We'll start helping out with things that need to be done here, and when we get home, we'll work on your garden," she said. "We'll become two garden sprites. We'll be nearly invisible, and we'll get the work done in a blink!"

That evening at dinner, the girls recounted everything that had happened over the past few days. They were especially delighted to share the news that Nathaniel would be living with the Tanakas.

"I'll have a friend to help me with my garden after Beckie's gone," Ana said.

Aunt Fannie smiled. "Such nice news," she

said. "A boy who needs a home, and two people with home that needs boy." She lifted a platter. "Now, a family celebration of our own. Who is ready for knishes? Our Beckie gets first choice, because she did the baking."

Rebecca hesitated. "I've already had a taste," she said, "so someone else can eat mine. Anyway, they just don't taste as good as the ones Aunt Fannie makes herself."

Ana placed a knish on her own plate and took one bite. Then she stood up abruptly. "I'll be right back—don't eat without me!" She dashed out the door, and Rebecca heard her thump down the stairs. In a flash, Ana returned clutching a handful of greens. She rinsed them quickly in the sink, chopped them on a plate, and sprinkled them over the knishes. "Try them now," she said, placing a knish on Rebecca's plate.

"What is it?" Rebecca asked.

"Green onions and parsley—from my garden!" Ana said proudly.

Rebecca took a bite, making sure to gather

lots of greens on her fork. The knish tasted a bit spicy, and as fresh as spring. It was delicious.

"We'll add these greens when we make another batch tomorrow," Ana said. "I'll peel the potatoes, and you cut them. Then I'll roll out the dough while you do the filling."

"I think you've finally found the missing ingredient," Rebecca declared. "Working together makes all the difference!"

Ana grinned at her, and Rebecca felt a smile curling up from her toes all the way to her face. Even a tsukumogami couldn't have made the week turn out any better.

LOOKING BACK

A PEEK INTO THE PAST

Children tending a large garden in New York City around 1900

When Rebecca and Ana were girls, many educators believed it was important for children to learn about nature—especially for children who lived in cities far from forests or farms. Some teachers were convinced that the best way for children to learn about nature was by growing food themselves. In Brooklyn, where Ana lived, a young schoolteacher named Ellen Eddy Shaw believed so strongly in this idea that she persuaded other teachers to give packets of vegetable seeds to their students.

Packets of seeds

Some children, like Ana, had access to small yards where they could plant the seeds they'd been given, but many didn't. Even 100 years ago, cities were crowded, bustling places, and space for gardens was hard to find. Families who wanted to grow food had to be resourceful. They planted seeds in discarded soap boxes and set seedlings to grow on tenement windowsills, fire escapes, or rooftops. Some went to vacant lots, where they snipped the leaves of wild plants such as dandelions and used them to make tasty salads and filling soups.

By 1914, Miss Shaw had been hired to work at the Brooklyn Botanic Garden, and she had a novel idea: the Botanic Garden could provide a space for children to plant their seeds and teach them how to care

Kids can still learn about gardening at the Brooklyn Botanic Garden today.

for their gardens. That first year, nearly 200 eager children applied for small plots on the garden

Girls in Rebecca's time work in a greenhouse at the Brooklyn Botanic Garden, planting seeds in pots of soil.

grounds. The 150 lucky young gardeners who received plots visited regularly to dig rows, sow seeds, and weed and water their vegetables. Their hard work was rewarded with a bountiful harvest of onions, carrots, beets, radishes, lettuce, beans, and other vegetables and fruits.

The Children's Garden still exists today, and more than a thousand children tend plots there every year. Each spring, they celebrate the start of the gardening season with a special Planting Day Parade.

Kids working in the Children's Garden today

An illustration of a Japanese woman wearing a kimono

Just as Ana was not alone in her passion for gardening, Rebecca was not alone in her fascination with Mrs. Tanaka's beautiful kimono, exquisite flower arrangements, and other aspects of Japanese culture and traditions. In the late 1800s and early 1900s, very few Americans had visited Japan. Many caught their first glimpse of traditional Japanese arts when they visited world fairs and exhibitions and saw displays showcasing Japanese architecture, garden design, and arts such as pottery and calligraphy. For visitors, it was love at first sight. The elegant, graceful designs of Japanese arts and crafts felt like a breath of fresh air compared with the dark and fussy designs people were used to at the time.

Americans loved Japanese design so much that they began buying Japanese-made products

Americans could see this Japanese teahouse and painted vase at the 1904 world's fair in St. Louis.

like fans, vases, and porcelain dishes for their homes. Art museums began displaying Japanese prints and paintings, and public gardens devoted large amounts of money and space to creating Japanese-style gardens. The Brooklyn Botanic Garden near Ana's apartment completed its Japanese Hill-and-Pond Garden in 1915. It was the first public Japanese garden in the country. Its creator, the landscape designer Takeo Shiota, said his goal was to design "a garden more beautiful than all others in the world."

A glimpse of Brooklyn's Japanese garden during Rebecca's time

Most of the features that Rebecca and Ana encounter in the story, including the shrine, the bridges, the teahouse, and the paths connecting them, can still be seen in the garden today.

The garden is also home to a bonsai tree collection, where more than 300 miniature trees are on display. And in spring, when hundreds of cherry trees burst into bloom in and around the garden, families stream there to stroll its paths, enjoy the serenity of the garden's design, and experience a world transformed for just a few short weeks by the magic of fragrance and color.

Scenes from the Japanese section of the Brooklyn Botanic Garden today, including a cherry tree in bloom (lower right)

Glossary

bonsai *(bohn-sigh)*—the Japanese art of growing miniature trees in containers or pots

boychik *(BOY-chik)*—an affectionate way to refer to a boy or young man in Yiddish

gefilte fish *(geh-FIL-tuh fish)*—a Yiddish term for a mixture of several types of fish, chopped and formed into balls and then cooked

hallah *(HAH-lah)*—a Hebrew word for a rich white bread made with eggs and usually braided

ikebana *(ee-keh-bah-nah)*—the Japanese art of making graceful arrangements of flowers, branches, and leaves in vases

Inari *(ee-nah-ree)*—the Japanese god of agriculture and fruitfulness

kimono *(kee-mo-no)*—a long robe with wide sleeves, usually tied with a wide sash. In the past, Japanese men, women, and children all wore kimonos.

knish *(kuh-NISH)*—in Yiddish, a food made of dough stuffed with a filling, such as potato, and then baked or fried

konnichiwa *(kohn-nee-chee-wah)*—a Japanese greeting that means hello or good afternoon

mitzvah *(MITS-vah)*—the Hebrew word for "command-ment." For Jews, it means a good deed, or the duty to perform acts of kindness.

rachmones *(rahk-MAHN-ehs)*—a Hebrew and Yiddish word that means compassion. It refers to giving mercy and understanding to ease someone's difficulty or pain.

spritz *(sprits)*—a Yiddish and German word that means to spray quickly and lightly with water

sushi *(soo-shee)*—a Japanese food made of cold rice formed into a ball, log, or other shape and topped or wrapped with pieces of raw seafood or vegetables

torii *(toh-ree)*—a gateway to a Japanese shrine, formed by two upright posts with a curved crosspiece connecting them

tsukumogami *(tsoo-koo-mo-ga-mee)*—in Japanese legends, a kind of sprite that lives in ancient tools and, if treated kindly, will do the tools' work for them

ABOUT THE AUTHOR

Jacqueline Dembar Greene is the author of the six books in the American Girl series about Rebecca Rubin. The books have won national awards, as have many of her numerous picture books and historical novels. Ms. Greene is also the author of several nonfiction books and two other Rebecca mysteries, *The Crystal Ball* and *Secrets at Camp Nokomis*.

In addition to writing, Ms. Greene enjoys gardening, hiking, biking, travel, and photographing the exotic places she visits.